A CLEAN SLATE

DAVID GARNETT

A CLEAN SLATE

HAMISH HAMILTON
LONDON

First published in Great Britain, 1971
by Hamish Hamilton Ltd.
90 Great Russell Street London WC1

Copyright © 1971 by David Garnett

SBN 241 02042 5

Printed in Great Britain by
Western Printing Services Ltd, Bristol

TO NERISSA

CHAPTER ONE

BILLY TONSON, the woman sitting at the table outside the café opposite the harbour at the easternmost end of Nice, attracted nobody's attention as she drank her Ricard and read her letters. She was tall and slim, wearing pale blue linen trousers, a sailcloth jumper with sandals on her bare feet. Her long hair, red-gold in colour, was twisted in a knot; her eyes very blue. When she opened her mouth, she showed sharp little eye-teeth, a front one was stopped with gold. The texture of her tanned face was that of a woman, not of a girl. She was forty-seven years old and wore lipstick, but no other make-up or eye shadow. The letters had been accumulating for the last week, while she was at sea. There was one from Sam, her husband, which she read first and there was one with a Dutch stamp, which would be from her old girl friend Hilda, which she left till last. Sam told her that his Burmese cat had had kittens and that they were pure-bred. Then there was one from the insurance people about her boat, The *Connie*—a small Bermuda rigged sloop, which ought to have been intercepted and dealt with by Sam's secretary, and then an invitation to spend the previous week-end at Moya's house in Antibes. 'That let's me out of that,' she murmured, and opened the one with the Dutch stamp. It had

I

been sent Express and had been waiting at the post office for three days. As she read it, she made a face and glared angrily across the table.

'Christ Almighty! What an unscrupulous bitch Hilda has become! Of course it's really Sam's fault for having let her worm my address out of him on the telephone.'

'God blast her!' Suddenly she looked at the dates in the letter again.

'Why the wretched boy is arriving at the airport in two hours time. I am in a spot.'

Hilda had written to say that her nephew David, an English schoolboy of seventeen, had been sent by his step-mother, who was suddenly remarrying, to spend the summer holidays with his Dutch cousins, but that they were all in bed with measles. So would Billy be an utter angel and take him for a cruise on the *Connie*? Sam seemed to think that she might like having a companion. And unless Hilda heard that the plan was impossible, she was sending him to Nice on the K.L.M. plane arriving at 14.00 hours, on Tuesday. It was now 12.20 Tuesday, 3rd August 1968.

Billy thrust her letters into her bag, paid for her Ricard and walked over to her Mini-Cooper Traveller with the left-hand drive, which she kept in France or Italy. The *Connie* was anchored in the harbour at Monte Carlo and she had driven over to get her letters and buy wine and provisions. It was lucky for the wretched boy that she hadn't sailed round, or he would have been left with no one to meet him.

Billy drove to the airport, only stopping on the way at

a sports shop to buy a complete second aqualung outfit, and, on an impulse, one of those lovely knives with horn handles made at La Guiole. A boy would like that.

She was there on time and standing at the custom's barrier, saw the little trickle of passengers descending the gangway. Among them was a young man—surely too tall and too old to be a schoolboy—looking about him expectantly. There was no other possible figure, so she waved at him and catching sight of her, he waved back. She supposed she must be the only person present to qualify as a friend of his aunt Hilda's.

When David Bruin came up to the passport and customs exit, Billy could see that he was dressed in a well cut dark suit and suède shoes and was bare-headed with dark hair. When, the next moment, they actually met and shook hands, she could see that he had very dark grey eyes and very white teeth, seen for a moment when he smiled at her greeting of: 'You're David aren't you? I'm Billy Tonson.'

It was the restraint in his manner that made him seem older—that and his good manners under which she thought she detected a shade of relief, which might mean a guarded approval at first sight.

They were clear of the customs and she directed the porter who carried David's suit-case and put it in the back of her car. She drove capably and well, paying attention to the traffic, but talking about his flight from Rotterdam.

'How lucky for me that cousin Hilda couldn't have you because her brats have all got measles. I'm all alone and I'm delighted to have a companion for a change. I hope you

3

like boats and can swim? I've taken up aqua lung diving.' As David was replying, she swung off the *Promenàde des Anglais* into a busy street behind it and soon slipped dextrously into a space big enough to take her car.

'Got to buy some food. Come along unless you're tired after your flight.' The boy did look tired and she wondered if perhaps he had been emotionally shocked by having discovered that he was unwanted in Sweden where his stepmother was suddenly getting married to a Swede. It was unfortunate she should marry in the first week of the summer holidays which David had expected to spend with her. Hilda had said that he had not been warned of the marriage and that he had arrived in Stockholm only to be shipped off to Holland. And after a lonely night in a hotel he had been put on a plane to go on a cruise with an unknown woman.

'I expect he is feeling like the girl in Carson McCullers' *A Member of the Wedding*, Hilda had added. Billy had not read the book or seen the play. But she must try and make his visit seem like an exciting adventure for them both. No doubt he was feeling baffled and angry at being disposed of as though he were still a child and, like an unwanted child, was in need of love, reassurance and consolation. That would have to wait until she saw how they got on. But in the circumstances his good manners won him high marks. He might so easily have been surly and bad-tempered. Meanwhile he was following her into a little pork butcher's and she was inspecting various *patés*.

'Do you like *rillettes*? Never tried them? Perhaps they are a bit greasy for eating at sea.' She passed on to a plate

4

of pigs' trotters and bought two. 'Tripe! Oh yes, let's have tripe. Felix says so few people know how good it is. Not that I'm much of a cook. Then two big sausages of salami because it keeps well and we may be out for a week.' She paid, plunged her purchases into a bag and led the way to a greengrocer's. Finally the bag was stuffed with tins of chestnut purée, a big carton of honey, butter, cheese, artichokes, salads, baby carrots and muscat grapes.

As they left the last shop—a dairy—she glanced at him and asked:

'You're not hungry, are you?' He was, and he admitted it.

'I thought they fed you on those planes.'

'I told the hostess I didn't want anything. You see I hadn't any money, only some travellers' cheques. Is there somewhere here where I can cash one?' Billy refrained from telling him that the lunch on the aeroplane was free and that the hostess probably would have changed an Express cheque. But his mistake made her realize how young and inexperienced he was.

'I'm hungry too. If we eat here I shall only have to cook an evening meal after we get back on board.' She led the way to a small dark room, where the last of the lunchers were leaving. David ate a faggot of asparagus, half a langouste and shared a bottle of white wine with Billy. After eating he looked better, but rather drunk, fell into a doze in the car and only woke up after they had stopped on the quay at Monte Carlo. He helped Billy load parcels into a motor dinghy and then got in and sat in the bows while she started the motor after which they chugged across the harbour to a five ton twenty-five foot sloop anchored inside the breakwater.

Although it was only four o'clock in the afternoon he went below and at her suggestion undressed and got into his bunk and fell fast asleep.

It was dark, the boat was in motion sliding almost noiselessly through the water except when a wave slapped the bow, or a rope creaked as the *Connie* heeled slightly to the wind. Billy was filled with a sense of adventure and amusement. What was this boy like who had accepted her as a companion and had gone off to sleep so naturally, without bothering to ask where they were bound?

He came on deck. 'I say where are we sailing?'

'Out to sea. What woke you up?'

'Would you mind telling me where I can find the lavatory?'

'Oh the loo is down below—on the left forward. But you can pee overboard—on the lee side.'

David went forward of the mast and disappeared behind the sail and had tucked himself tidy when he reappeared.

'You had better eat,' said Billy. 'There is hot soup in the thermos, bread, paté, butter and cheese, some green figs and wine. I ate before casting off, because with all this traffic about, I can't leave the cockpit for long. When you've eaten, pack the dishes up in the racks so they won't smash if the wind gets up.'

'By the way,' she added 'I bought you a knife. I thought

6

you might like it.' Billy noticed that David's expression changed and she guessed it was because he thought that she had bought him a present suitable for a small boy. She hastily pulled the knife out of her pocket and added: 'A good knife is indispensable when one is sailing and these French knives are made of soft steel and much easier to keep really sharp.'

David took the knife and looked at it.

'But it is most beautiful. It's a really lovely thing. How much do I owe you for it?'

'Don't be absurd. I bought it to give you. It's just like the one I always carry myself. I have a thing about these knives.'

'Thank you most awfully. It is the most beautiful present I have ever been given. I don't know why you are so kind to me,' said David pocketing the knife. He went down into the cabin.

Billy steered and thought her visitor over. He was a bit formal and stiff, but he had very good manners. She had been afraid either of a small boy who would be difficult to look after and keep from falling overboard, or an oaf who would make himself very much at home while making her aware that she was one of the despised older generation, revenging himself because he was generally unwanted. He was, moreover, marvellously good-looking and old for his age. Billy remembered that his father, Augustine Bruin, had been a handsome man. Hilda had been desperately in love with him but he had married her elder sister and then she had married that boring Dutchman.

Well, David might so easily have been a little toad

covered with spots, or have had huge ears that stuck out. She sighed deeply. She had never had and never would have, a child. And now for a couple of weeks she would know what it was like to have a son. With a certain eagerness she thought of teaching him to handle a sailing boat and aqualung diving.

Her thoughts became dreamy and took odd directions as she grew sleepy and she came to herself with a start to find that the object of them was standing close to her. He was in his pyjamas.

'You'll get cold, come in here.' When Billy opened the blanket to make room for him, he could see that she was still dressed. He sat down rather primly beside her and she folded the blanket round them both. Her body was warm.

'How are you steering?' he asked.

'I don't have to do much. The *Connie* steers herself in a steady wind. If she falls off I shall shift the tiller lines a little. But watch the compass in the binnacle,' and she began to explain about setting it. But soon she saw that he was not listening. She had wrapped him round in the blanket and pressed his body close to hers simply to keep him warm. But very soon she became aware that the boy was melting with physical desire for her. He was shivering with embarrassment and longing, not with cold. He made a little movement trying to shift away, but the blanket held him close. Then he began to breathe faster and Billy was certain that his cock, so close to her, was standing up straight and stiff and that his desire was getting out of control. Unless she did something abrupt to change the situation, she would be putting one arm round his neck

8

and touching it with her other hand while the *Connie* might fall off, and there would be salt water aboard. All that would never do.

'What an old baby-snatcher I am,' she thought to herself. Then she said aloud: 'You had better get back to bed,' flung the blanket wide and for a moment all was revealed. In the next David had scrambled away clutching his pyjamas. She smiled wondering whether he was persuading himself that she hadn't seen. Then she heard him below and water running. Later she left the *Connie* to steer herself and went down into the cabin.

'Have you everything you want, David?' she asked in a kind voice.

'Oh yes, thanks.'

'We'll go diving tomorrow. We are going to have a wonderful time together,' she said coming in and sitting down on his bunk. Her hand strayed dangerously near the centre of the blanket.

'I didn't come down to do this' she told herself and stood up. She wanted to bend over and kiss him, but he would think she was being maternal, so she just smiled at him and went away.

In that curious silver kingdom below the waves they looked questioningly at each other. She saw a slim naked boy wearing only a triangle and of course his bubbling mask and the tubes and pack of air cylinders. She could not see his eyes, but could tell that he was staring at her,

9

perhaps he had never seen a woman's body so close. She knew that she was splendidly fit and flat-bellied, with firm breasts under her bikini. But she had forgotten that her mane of long hair streamed upwards from her scalp like the wavering of a flaming torch, transmuted from its natural golden brown to silvery grey at the bottom of the sea. In and about the vertical cone of silver hair, rose the escaping bubbles from her mask. Through the window he could have seen her shadowy eyes.

David turned away and began to search the bottom of the sea for what he could find. He was standing on firm sand and there was less to be seen than could be found on a beach. Once he had become familiar with the light and the pressure of the water and the almost weightlessness, so that his feet barely rested on the sea floor and left no imprints on the sand, there was nothing to look at. A moment later Billy touched him on the shoulder and pointed upwards. Then taking him by both hands she kicked off the bottom and each gave a few kicks which brought them almost to the surface. Billy had been looking upwards and gave a wriggle and a side-kick which brought them within reach of the boat with its little ladder rolling first away out of the water and then dipping nearer to them. Billy pushed him towards it and while he held it she took the clip off his nose, afterwards releasing herself and following him up the ladder.

She went below and called up to him: 'Chambéry or Dubonnet?"

'I've never tasted either, choose for me,' said David shyly. All the toughness which was part of being a sailor woman, navigating her own boat, cruising single-handed often out of sight of land for days at a time, melted, dissolved at the sound of that shy voice and she herself felt a throb of something so unbearably sensitive that it could not be exposed, as though she were a snake that had suddenly sloughed its skin. It was agony to feel again, even for a split second, as she had first felt when she was twelve years old. She turned her face away, poured out two glasses in silence and then handed him one. It was lovely to have a boy looking at her like that. Her skin tingled under his eyes.

'Which is it?' he asked.

'Which is what?' she asked confused.

'What drink have you given me?'

'Oh Chambéry, I expect,' she replied vaguely.

They lay side by side on the fore deck. Ordinarily Billy would have bared the whole of her body to the sun but the effect of David's voice and of the ardent curiosity of his look, was to make her wrap herself tighter. But David soon turned on his face and was roasting the whole of his naked back in the sun. The sea was too salt: the sun was too hot and pleasure came from the extremes.

They made efforts to locate a wreck which had been marked on her map. They could not however find it, but they did come across a strange heap of squared stones thickly covered in weed on the sea floor which they decided were blocks of marble. Not a very rewarding discovery.

During these four days Billy was happier than she had been for two or three years. Every moment of the day was occupied by providing pleasures for David and in looking after his needs. While he fell asleep in the sun after their morning dive, she would go below and turn her hand to trying to cook a bouillabaisse or a piperàde. She threw away the tripe as it remained like rubber. She had never bothered to cook anything but porridge, or fry a fish when she was alone.

David always asked for more and Billy who had all her life been abstemious and indifferent to food, felt a childish delight and pleasure in filling his plate. They slept side by side on deck in the afternoon. If the sun were too hot, Billy would rise silently and shift the awning so as to shade David while he slept. And then she would tiptoe back and lie down beside him and listen to his breathing and that was an absorbing happiness.

'We shall have to go into port tomorrow,' she said as they ate their evening meal on the fourth day. 'I've nothing left but a few tins. We'll make for Nice tomorrow and load up with enough meat and wine, vegetables and fruit to last us for a week. Then we'll go down the coast of Italy.'

'Why are we going back to France first?' asked David.

'The chief thing is to buy wine. I shall stock up the boat because Felix says one can never be sure of Italian wine. And there may be some letters for me in Nice.'

The anchor chain rattled out as the *Connie* swung and David had just finished making it fast, when he saw a small boat coming towards them. There was a boatman in the stern and a short thick-set plump man with red cheeks sitting on the thwart. The boatman cut his motor and laid hold of the fender hanging over the side. Billy who was down below could hear the conversation.

'Is Billy aboard?'

'Lady Tonson is below,' answered David stiffly.

'She's not ill, is she?'

'No. She is changing into shore clothes,' said David.

'I'll come aboard then. Give me a hand.' David turned away to the companion and called down.

'There's a man here wants to come aboard.' But when he turned back the stranger was already on deck. He brushed past him and dived below.

'Felix darling!' Billy's voice rose in a roar of welcome. There was the sound of a noisy kiss and Billy saying:

'Well, you've caught me with my pants off this time.'

When Billy followed her visitor on deck she noticed a sulky look on David's face and was not surprised when he refused Felix's invitation to come ashore, saying that he would much prefer to stay on the *Connie* and look after her.

There was something shut and desperate in his voice that she had not heard before, so she did not add her persuasion to Felix's when he touched the boy on the shoulder and said: 'Oh come along. I want to give you two a really good dinner and we can make plans for the future.'

Instead she said 'Promise to keep a good look out for me and be ready to fetch me off in the dinghy. I shall be on the quay with a taxi load of wine and food in about two hours' time.'

Secretly she was delighted by that sulky look. David was jealous. It was ridiculous. It was awfully stupid. But she felt pleased and flattered.

'You must have dinner with me. I insist on that,' said Felix.

'Shopping comes first. We'll settle about dinner afterwards,' and with that Billy climbed into the waiting shore boat, Felix followed her, the boatman started the engine and they swung in a circle for the shore. Two hours later Billy stood on the quay and waved. She was alone surrounded with bags and cases. She was relieved to see David draw up the dinghy and get into it. She had been afraid that he might have gone below to sulk.

'I was afraid you wouldn't be watching for me,' she said and began handing down her purchases: three cases of wine, one of Vichy water, a sack of vegetables, a lot of meat and bread and fruit.

'It was lucky I saw you. I wasn't sure that you were coming back,' David said, but Billy did not reply. The engine popping, as she revved it up, made conversation difficult.

'We'll stow everything away and make all shipshape and ready to sail before we go ashore again.'

'Go ashore?' asked David.

'Yes, I've accepted an invitation for both of us to have dinner with Felix and some friends of his tonight. But this is a secret which you mustn't let out. I am planning to sail in the early hours after we get back on board. I think if we

14

leave it, some of them might ask to come with us and that would be a dreadful bore.' David said nothing.

'Felix is a darling and supposed to be one of the best cooks in the world, but I don't care that much for food and more than a few hours of his company drives me round the bend.'

'I thought he was your lover,' said David.

Billy gazed at him, haughty and surprised, not that he should have imagined such a thing, but that he should have the hardihood to say so. She had been to bed with Felix once or twice, so she did not deny the possibility, but only said, after a pause:

'Actually he's a queer.' Then: 'Come on, work to be done.' She started up the auxiliary motor.

'Are we going to cut the dinner after all?' asked David.

'No, I'm taking her alongside the quay. We must fill our freshwater tank before we slip off on a cruise.'

Billy brought the *Connie* gently alongside the quay. David leapt off and slipped the loop of the hawser over a bollard. Five minutes later a black plastic pipe was filling the tank. David went below, washed and put on his best suit. After Billy had taken the *Connie* out again and had changed her clothes, they set out for the restaurant where they were to meet Felix Hotchkiss and his friends. There were three of them: Roma Palgrave, a thin woman with an ironical, twisted mouth, Gundred a girl with long straight straw coloured hair and a loud voice and Derek Hughes a handsome young man who had just returned from Morocco.

Billy began talking to the boy and girl, but watched

15

while Felix pressed David to take a Pernod. She guessed it was in the hopes that he would dislike it and make a face. But David seemed to like the taste of aniseed, drank it up and asked for another and then for a third.

When they sat down to dinner, Billy thought he looked a bit vague. At dinner David sat between Roma and Gundred and Billy opposite. To her surprise he began talking and Billy heard him say:

'No. I usually feel repulsion for other people. Human beings always betray each other. They think it's amusing. I prefer animals—wild animals—and I feel no fear of them. I know I am safer with them. If I met a lioness in the desert, or a tigress in the jungle, I would go straight up to her and make friends and that friendship would be more worth having than with any man or with any woman. I once made friends with a boaconstrictor and he trusted me completely. He was taken out of his cage and put in my arms and he looked me in the eyes and touched my lips with his tongue. He knew the difference between me and every one else. One day I shall go back and break the lock of his cage and carry him away to live with me.'

'Where do you propose to live?' asked Gundred.

'Somewhere in the jungle.'

'I think you've been reading Kipling, haven't you? I can't endure him myself,' said Roma.

'Oh I have read the *Jungle Books* and *Kim*. Actually I was born in India and I believe that I was a wolf child that my father adopted. Only my supposed parents are dead, so I shall never find out.' There was a complete silence round the table. Then David looked round, examining them all

16

and went on: 'You know of course that I am afraid of you
—of all of you. But I have no fear of wild animals. I read
a book about a boy in the West Indies who made friends
with a shark. I am hoping to meet one when I am diving,
so that I can do the same. When I meet a dolphin I shall
ride on his back. You couldn't do that, could you?' he
ended, glaring across the table at Felix.

'I think it's most unlikely,' said Felix laughing. David
lapsed into silence and the others talked among themselves till the end of dinner. Then Billy saw David drink
up the brandy set before him and hold out his glass for
more. Billy made a movement to interfere, but thought
better of it and David looking across the table at her said:
'I may be only a schoolboy but I won't let anyone play
with me,'. . . There was a dead silence. Then Roma said
very sweetly in her slightly foreign accent:

'But that's very unkind of you. If I saw more of you I
should feel very much tempted. I am a bit of a wolf-child
too, a *lupa*.' The others burst into laughter.

'I am going back to the boat,' said David. He stood
up with difficulty, pushed back his chair, wavered and
said:

'Tomorrow I'm going to ride a doffin and then hitch-
hike home.' He took a step, tripped and fell. Felix and
Derek Hughes helped Billy get David back on board and
down below on to his bunk. Soon after she had taken
them ashore and said good-bye and hauled the dinghy up
and fastened it down on the forehatch, she started up the
motor and took the *Connie* out to sea before the first light.
There was a fair wind and an oily swell and she could hear

David vomiting as she hoisted the mainsail. She had too much to think about without attending to his needs. He would have to be sick anyway, even if he weren't at sea, and the sooner he got it done with the better. She had plenty of time to wonder about his behaviour as she held the little boat to her course in rising wind and sea.

She could not believe that it had all arisen on her account. He didn't care enough for her to be more than momentarily jealous.

It was due to an inferiority complex, arising from being thought a schoolboy in a slightly equivocal situation with regard to a much older woman. Also a desire to impress by boasting—though that story of the boa constrictor sounded as though it had a basis of truth. Bolting off that series of pernods, even without the greasy food and wine and brandy that followed, was enough to explain it. There was however an aggressiveness about his behaviour which worried her. She hoped he was not going to be one of those unfortunate men who always become quarrelsome in their cups. And then she thought how absolutely sweet he was —how divine of him to imagine himself a wolf-child! She loved him. There was no doubt about that.

Meanwhile he would have to lie there vomiting because she could not leave the deck. Wind and sea rose and, as dawn broke, she could see white horses everywhere.

Billy loved matching herself against rough weather and the hours passed and David was forgotten, as every little while a huge wave came and the *Connie* slid down and down and down and Billy held her and edged her up and water hit her with a last spiteful slash and then they were clear and the seas pouring off the deck and Billy was watching for the next. Hours went by. The sun had probably set. It was almost dark when Billy saw David push his way out on deck. She hailed him.

'Good boy. Better now? I hope so because I want you to take the tiller. I'm getting a bit stiff.'

She had been steering the ship for seventeen hours while he had been lying below retching and pitying himself for his hangover. He made his way to the cockpit and silently took the tiller.

'Keep her a few points East of South and if you see a big one coming, take it absolutely head on.' Billy climbed out of the cockpit, lashed David so he couldn't be carried away and went down below. She was surprised and gratified to find that he had made an effort to clean up beside his bunk. She would tackle it later on. But that could wait. She made a pot of tea, filled a thermos with it and took it up to David.

'Do you all the good in the world and swallow a couple of these.' She gave him two Kwells tablets and went below and drank a bowl of strong tea with a lot of sugar, laced with whisky. Then she lay down and went straight off to sleep knowing that unless the boy lost his head, the *Connie* was unlikely to come to serious harm. Being in sole charge of her would do him more good than anything in the world.

Billy had lowered the mainsail and the *Connie* was running under a reefed staysail with the auxiliary motor at slow—just enough to keep steerage way upon her. She fell asleep and was only uneasily brought half awake when the

Connie went under and took longer than usual to shake herself free of the sea.

When she woke up, she went first to clean up the mess by David's bunk, making a really good job of it and throwing the cabin carpet overboard as it would always stink. Then she made coffee and cooked breakfast and ate it and, only after that, did she go and speak to David who looked at her without interest. He seemed to have become an automaton watching the waves.

'The worst of the storm is over. The wind is dropping. I've made breakfast. There's coffee and eggs and bacon. While you have a rest I'll take over. Thank you David. You've done well.'

As he climbed out of the cockpit he almost lost his balance and might have gone overboard, if Billy had not grabbed him. He had forgotten the speech which he had rehearsed earlier that night. So he said nothing but lowered his body carefully down the companion and was lost to view.

CHAPTER TWO

THE weather continued stormy with hot sun, clear cloud-less skies and a blustering squally South Wind—the ill-famed sirocco. Billy ran for shelter to the Gulf of Spezia and anchored well off shore, within sight of the strange little town of Porto Venere where Greek and Roman sailors used to land to pay homage to Venus—and to enjoy the priestesses of her temple, which has been replaced by the Christians with a Church dedicated to Saint Lawrence, who is portrayed above its doorway grilling on his gridiron.

During the first day, the weather kept the bay fairly free of pleasure craft. But by midday next morning the sea was full of all sorts of motor boats, sailing dinghies, catamarans with outboard motors and curious contraptions which pro-gressed with a paddle wheel worked with bicycle pedals, chain and gears. The *Connie* attracted interest and in the late afternoon they were continually being hailed by nautically attired figures who sometimes let their speed-boats drift unpleasantly close, before opening up their engines and dashing off, leaving a wake that made the wine slop from a full glass. Then the rough weather came back and the bay was free of pleasure boats. The sky was clear, the sun hot and through the binoculars they could see that the beaches were covered with human bodies and the patches of road that were visible, were packed with crawling cars. They were glad to be at sea though the *Connie* pitched and rolled uncomfortably as they rode at anchor and it was a relief to slip into the peaceful silver kingdom beneath the waves. They hoped to find relics on the sea bed, nor were they entirely disappointed, for there were bottles and wine-jars of all ages and David even found the neck of an amphora with one of the handles unbroken, among the broken chianti flasks.

They stayed down longer than usual and David went up first. Billy followed, but when she surfaced, David was not there.

For a second she wondered if he could be on the other side of the boat's hull, then she dived and saw bubbles and almost at once caught sight of him below her. She struck out with her frog flippers and caught him before he reached the bottom. He was limp and she swam up with him, seeing, as she did so, that his mask had been displaced. When she had got his body to the surface, she had to pass a rope round it, then climb the ladder. This took a little while, because the *Connie* was rolling in the slow waves. Once on board, she got hold of the rope and by main strength lifted him half out of the water. With the next roll she was able to drag him further on board and finally got him out on deck. The pitching hull, or the ladder, must have hit him as he surfaced, for his mask had been smashed. Billy pulled it off and after pressing all the water she could out of him, put her lips to his and began to breathe in and out as she had been trained when learning the technique of 'the kiss of life'.

22

There was blood running from a cut on David's temple. But she felt and thought very little, for she was fighting and was physically exhausted herself, though unaware of it. After half an hour, David opened his eyes: he had begun breathing and his pulse was perceptible. His body was cold and Billy lifted him and dragged him down the companion and laid him on her bunk, covered him with blankets then, still naked, she slipped in beside his cold body to warm it with her own.

He went on breathing, she pressed his body close, kissing him and then began to sob uncontrollably.

She was still sobbing when David showed signs of being sick and she recovered her control to attend to him. Afterwards she gave him some brandy. He opened his eyes and looked about him vaguely. Then fell back, too exhausted to wonder where he was, or what had happened. Billy watched and seeing he was sleeping, slipped in again beside him, so that she could watch him close. Half an hour later she was asleep herself.

The wind had dropped. The *Connie* rode at anchor on an even keel and the sun sent shafts of light through the cabin portholes. Billy woke and felt David moving. One of her naked breasts was pressed against his body the other free. She saw him moisten his lips. He was breathing fast and was lifting the blanket to look under it at her body, still unaware that she was awake. Then she moved slightly and he looked up to see her smiling at him.

They lay looking into each other's eyes, not speaking or moving. Billy could see a look of intense desire and timidity on David's face and smiled mischievously, enjoying playing with and teasing this inexperienced boy. She felt his body tauten and his cock throbbing against her belly. She knew she must help him, because he was still little more than a child. But first she said: 'I want to look at you,' and pulled the blanket off and dropped it on the floor beside the divan.

David put his hand over his cock but Billy said:

'Don't be silly. I like looking at your body. I love that cock of yours. Do you like what you see of me?'

As she spoke David began to tremble, the blood rushed to his head and he made a movement as though to throw himself upon her.

Then shifting her position she opened her legs, moistened her hand with saliva and put it down, taking hold of his cock to guide it, but before letting it come in, she rubbed the head for a little while high up in the cleft, then giving a sigh put it down lower and it slipped into her at once and she felt David trembling. She gasped with delight, kissed David's mouth and then lay loose and passive while he began to ride her and his cock was like a rod of soft fire.

'Harder, harder, faster, faster,' she whispered and David gave swift violent strokes and suddenly a scream of pleasure and she came too and gave a strangled scream and felt that she was flooded inside and went on coming and lay gripping his cock tight, trying to keep it for as long as she could. David growled at her and then lay quite still, until, with his erection gone, his cock slipped out and he turned on his back. Billy gave a little moan at his going and put her hand down to touch the little sticky wet thing, but David brushed her hand away and almost the next moment she saw that he was asleep. Because he was asleep, he was especially precious, a boy more precious to her than any of the men with whom she had lain. At that moment Billy, who had already saved David from drowning and restored him to life, would have made any sacrifice for him. She would have thrown herself into fire as unthinkingly as she had swum down into the sea, she would have allowed her bones to be broken, her body crushed, her limbs torn asunder.

She looked with worship at his skin already turning gold from the sun, at the long dark lashes resting on his cheeks and noted the few beads of sweat that had broken just below them, and on his forehead and his upper lip. David was a God and Billy who was unaccustomed to worship God except in the fury of a storm at sea, worshipped David.

'I can do this because I'm not his mother—and yet I feel exactly as I imagine a mother would feel. Do mothers have incestuous desire for their sons?' Billy asked herself this, and then looking at David, forgot all in a wave of such joy and happiness that for a little while words meant nothing. Later she said out loud, perhaps because if she heard her own words spoken they became more true than if she only thought them:

'You belong to me now . . . It had to be . . . after all I saved your life and now I take my reward. You belong to me.'

David who had been lying apparently unconscious, with his head against her right breast, opened his eyes and asked:

25

'Saved my life? What happened? I can't remember anything. What happened? I was coming up from a dive. And then, wasn't I sick? And then . . .'

'The bows of the boat must have crashed down onto your head as you came up and your mask was knocked off. When I came up, you weren't anywhere to be seen. So I dived and got hold of you before you got to the bottom. I had a job hauling you on board. After that I blew air into your lungs and pushed it out again for ages and ages. At last you came to life and I dragged you down here and got into bed with you to keep you warm.'

'So you really did save my life.' David took hold of her shoulders and gazed at her in astonishment.

'You mean to say that I should be dead now, but for you?' Billy nodded and choked back tears.

'I'm not going to let you play about at the bottom of the sea again. I want to keep you alive.'

'Am I alive enough now?' asked David and she felt his cock harden against her groin.

'More, more, harder, faster.'

And when at last he came again after taking his full time, they were not two bodies but one. Flesh and spirit in each were fused and ran like streams of molten metal into a new mould.

Later, David's fingers stroking her breast and the small of her back, left lines so sensitive that she imagined them luminous with phosphorescent fire.

.   .   .

There was a hoarse voice hailing them. Billy slid off the bunk, grabbed her burnous and went on deck. A fisherman was holding on to the ladder. Seeing her he held up a live octopus which gazed from unseeing lack-lustre eyes, while its eight arms writhed round its captor's forearm, like the serpents on the Laocoon.

Billy agreed to buy some fish, but while she was bargaining the fisherman began to stroke the calf of her leg so she called down the companion way:

'Our visitor is getting enterprising. Call out something so that he knows I'm not alone.'

'What the hell is going on up there? Tell the wop to bugger off,' shouted David angrily in English and the fisherman, hearing an angry male voice, cast off from the ladder, blew Billy a kiss and putting his motor in gear went off with a popping of the exhaust.

'Look what I've got,' she said showing the dinghy bailer half full of greyish, semi transparent, baby cuttlefish. 'Felix ought to be here to cook the things.'

'Be damned to your bloody Felix,' said David. And she laughed with pleasure, 'All right be damned to him. But I don't know how to cook the things.' However she grated a crust, beat up an egg and dipped the little cuttlefish in egg and bread crumbs and then fried them in oil. They were delicious and they ate every one, and went on to finish the meal with bread and goat cheese, all washed down with a white dry Burgundy. Then she made coffee in the Italian machine with Italian coffee.

The weather had changed to fair. That afternoon they landed at Porto Venere, made their vows to Aphrodite on the site of her temple, and bought a supply of fresh vegetables, fruit and fish. David also sent off postcards to his Dutch aunt and his housemaster. To the latter he wrote: 'Have just worshipped at the shrine of Venus,' which he knew would please the old latinist. He did not say with what rites the worship had been performed. A third postcard, addressed to his friend Brian Milburne, he showed to Billy. She read:

'Rose from the dead and am greatly enjoying my resurrection', and they laughed together.

That night David began to play with one of her nipples, but Billy took his hand and put it down between her legs.

'Touch me very gently just in there—a little higher—can you feel a little thing—some people call it 'the man in the boat'—if you touch it very gently you give me intense pleasure and make me want you—and the whole thing.' And Billy slipped down in the bed to find his cock already standing up stiffly. She kissed it, licking round the head of it with her tongue and then taking it all into her mouth until David cried out: 'No. No. No more.' David was still lying on his back as she climbed back to him.

'Let me come on top, this time,' she said and then knelt on him with her thighs apart. Then wetting her hand with saliva, she took hold of his cock and guided it in, then leaning back, straining his cock against her clitoris while she sat upright on him.

David lay passive gazing at the lean brown body with the breasts ivory tipped with rose. He put up a hand and touched a nipple. Billy bent down over him saying: 'Don't be shy take it in your mouth.' He sucked first one and then the other and Billy felt her breasts swell and tauten and then she sat upright again and began an up and down motion, sometimes almost bouncing on him until suddenly he could endure passive pleasure no more and began lifting his pelvis and thrusting up into her. Billy let herself fall on him and her long tawny gold hair fell over his face and blinded him. David thrust harder, then putting his hands down, gripped her buttocks and held her hard and close, as he drove his cock further and further into her until Billy began to cry and sob and as she came in a flood, she felt David come too and he gave a cry almost of anguish.

Later she said to him: 'We were two wild animals in the Jungle that time.'

David looked at her with a happy, completely exhausted smile.

'You won't kill me, will you?'

Billy shook her head and tossed her hair back so that it fell over his naked shoulders.

'I once read about Buddha,' said Billy. 'He was a prince in India but he could remember his previous incarnations and told his bride that she had been a tigress and he a tiger and that they had made love many times together in the jungle.'

'You are certainly a tigress,' said David.

'You are more like a young lion. I believe that lions do mate with tigresses sometimes,' said Billy.

'We know that they do,' said David. 'Now I'm going for a swim while you cook the supper.'

'Let's sail down to Sicily,' said Billy next morning as they drank their coffee.

The fickle and treacherous sea was showing itself in a different mood. The sun was shining, waves sparkling and wind fair on the quarter. David raised the anchor while Billy hauled up the sails and they left the narrow mouth of the gulf of Spezia and set sail South, while the great cliffs and rocks receded over the left quarter of the stern. The weather continued perfect and they coasted for four days down the Tyrrhenian sea, passing Elba, sighting Ischia and then passing through the straits between Procida and the mainland. But though the weather was perfect, something began to go wrong between them.

David spent the whole day watching the flying fish and tried to measure the distance they covered scudding over the rippling sea and he became so obsessed by them, talking of nothing else, that Billy was annoyed, bored, almost jealous. At night, fortunately, flying fish weren't visible and Billy and he often slept together, while the balance of sail and rudder lines which could not be trusted in a gale, kept them on their set course.

But while David seemed to have his mind occupied only by the distance that a flying fish could scud over the waves —he swore it was often a hundred and fifty yards—Billy was tormented by a more personal problem.

She had asked David about his life and he had told her freely about his childhood, when he was carted about in the Indian jungles on his father's archaeological expeditions to discover buried cities and temples. And then about his prep. school days and his father's second marriage and death, only a year before, and about his stepmother.

But he had apparently accepted Billy as a woman without a past, like Athene sprung fully-formed from the head of Zeus. It never seemed to occur to him to ask her about her life, her marriages, previous love affairs, or how she came to be sailing about alone in the Mediterranean sea. The only personal remark he had made was when he had supposed that Felix Hotchkiss was her lover. And as he did not ask questions, Billy did not volunteer information. Yet one day David must meet her husband Sam, and she wanted them to like each other. She had not concealed David's existence from Sam: she had written two long letters about him, and a third was waiting to be posted from Naples, explaining her prolonged absence. But a curious shyness, or cowardice, inhibited the mention of Sam's name, and explaining the circumstances of her marriage, to David. Whenever she came near to the subject, something would crop up to prevent the long painful and complicated exposition. Billy hated complications. She believed that all human relationships were really simple. But in this case she was making her final explanations far more complicated for she was leading David to believe that she was a rich woman with no ties.

He did not ask her personal questions for a reason that she was not to find out until later. All his life he had been short of money. His father had always spent every penny on archaeology. When he died David had inherited nothing and was aware that his food, clothes and schooling and the five pounds a month pocket money, were paid by his pretty stepmother.

Now chance had made him the guest of a rich woman. He had always resented being dependent. In the case of his

31

stepmother the resentment was of long standing and bitter. She would tease him about not going to the theatre, without offering to buy tickets for him, when she must have known that he had not the money to go. And he never asked her for any.

Billy's hospitality and generosity was more acceptable, because it had come by chance and was offered so freely. But in itself it was repugnant. He had been tempted to ask her:

'Where does the money come from to pay for the bread and the wine and the harbour dues? To what detergent, household convenience, or missile am I indebted for this holiday?'

But he suppressed these questions, just as Billy suppressed the exposition of her married life and of her past. These suppressions came between them and spoilt the spontaneity of their love-making.

'I am a gigolo—I have become a gigolo without knowing it,' David said to himself and the thought made him turn away roughly after the act of love, at the moment when Billy was clinging to him and most vulnerable.

'I am enjoying David's love on false pretences,' Billy said to herself as she sought new ways of arousing and satisfying his desire.

Before they reached Naples these concealments resulted in a quarrel.

'Naples may be the last place where you can buy clothes for some time. You need a couple of those striped singlets, another pair of cotton trousers and some rope-soled shoes. And perhaps a straw hat to shade your eyes. Here's twenty

32

thousand lire. I should think that would about cover
it.'

David shook his head angrily: 'No thanks. I don't
want anything.'

'Well, take the note in case you see something you want
to buy while you are on shore.'

'I don't want to take any money, thank you,' said David.

'Please don't be so silly. I've got masses of money and I
love you and want to give you things.'

'No thanks.'

'Well don't look so fierce. Come and make love to me,
you pig-headed boy.'

David set upon her and practically raped her and when
he came after a dozen violent thrusts, he pushed her away,
zipped up his flies and staggered to his feet.

There was a long silence.

'That was brutal. You hurt me David. I hoped I taught
you how to make love. What you have done was cruel and
insulting.'

'You can put me ashore at Naples and find another
young boy and teach him to satisfy you better.'

Billy leapt to her feet and hit David on the mouth
cutting his lip. He glowered at her and went on deck. They
did not speak to each other again as they motored in to
Naples harbour and Billy brought the *Connie* alongside the
wall of the yacht harbour. David waiting on deck, jumped
on shore, slipped the loop of the cable over a bollard and
without looking back walked off into the town.

Billy did not like to leave the *Connie*. There are thieves
in every port and she had heard that the Neapolitans had a

33

reputation for being thievish. At last she found a dock policeman, put her case to him and was told that she would be quite safe if she engaged an old fellow whom he pointed out, to watch the boat all the morning for five hundred lire. So she went off marketing. She was unable to decide what to do about David if he did not come back. She searched his cabin and found that he had taken his passport and travellers cheques—they amounted to about nine pounds—so she guessed that he intended to leave her and hitch-hike home.

If he did not come back by the following morning she thought she would sail away—either to Sicily—or back to Monaco. She decided it would be better not to go to the police. David was young and strong and except about money, wasn't a fool. He was old enough to be responsible for himself. It cost Billy a lot of worry to make this decision and then to stick to it. Naples was full of criminals who might rob him, or stick a knife in his back and throw his body into the cellar of an empty house. But it was more likely that a kindly lorry driver would give him a lift to Rome. In the meantime she went on with routine preparations for continuing the voyage: filling up the tanks with fresh water and with diesel oil, buying bread, fresh vegetables, salami, tins of milk, and wine said to be grown on the slopes of Vesuvius.

Late that evening she was still stowing away her purchases, when she heard the old watchman ask a challenging question and David's voice attempting an answer in Italian. He came down into the saloon, looked at Billy and asked: 'Do you know where the dettol is?'

'Here it is. What do you want it for?' David took it silently.

'Has someone stuck a knife into you? I had better have a look.'

'I want to wash my cock. I've been with a prostitute. At least I suppose she was one.'

Billy felt violently angry. His words were like a blow in the face. But she would not have shown her anger without feeling contempt for herself, and the immediate effect of David's words was to freeze all expression of emotion in Billy. She did not flinch.

'I'll come and wash you and do it properly,' she said perfectly calmly.

She poured a little dettol into a mug, added water until it was only slightly milky and then while David held up his shirt, she swabbed his parts thoroughly with a wash rag dipped in the disinfectant and then pressed open the lips of the urethra and held his cock in the mug.

'How long ago did you go with her?'

'Not more than three quarters of an hour' he replied.

'I don't think there's the slightest danger,' she said.

'I shan't ever be able to make love to you again,' said David in a strange frightened voice.

'Is that why you did it?' asked Billy and immediately regretted having spoken. A wound that could never be made whole was better not admitted, or discussed. For almost as strong as her anger, was the wish to conceal from David how much he had hurt her.

'No. No. No. Don't be so unjust as to think that. I . . . I'll explain . . .'

35

'Tell me about it later on. I want to cast off and get out of the harbour before dark.'

'I was going to ask you to lend me the money for the railway fare home. I'll repay it when I get back to England. I cashed my cheques but I hadn't nearly enough and since then I've given Virginia five thousand lire.'

An hour later they were sailing past Vesuvius in the darkness, Billy steering and David sitting beside her in the cockpit. Billy put up the lights and brought up a supper of bread and cheese and wine and mortadella and a melon. When they had eaten, she said:

'Well I see you are wanting to tell me all about your adventure.'

'Your trying to give me money made me very angry. I'm only a schoolboy with an allowance of five pounds a month. I thought if I took money from you I should feel like a prostitute!' Billy made a movement as though to speak but thought better of it. Presently David went on: 'That's why I behaved in that beastly way when you asked me to make love to you. After that, I thought it was all over and that I would cash my cheques and either hitch-hike or take the train home. I only had eight pounds, it came to ten thousand lire and a few bits over. I tried to find out where the truck drivers start from on the way up to Rome. But I must have gone the wrong way. At last I got into a very crowded street and was thinking I had better get something to eat, when a girl in a green velvet dress came past and looked at me. She wasn't much older than I am and had a very beautiful face. I asked her where I could eat and she led me through a very dirty alley to an old house, with swarms of children playing on the steps and then led me up the stairs to her room at the top. She fished a huge old key from out of her bosom and unlocked the door and directly we had gone in, she locked it from the inside. It was a big dirty room with a bed and a pail and a little cupboard, but no table or chairs. There was a picture of Christ washing a woman's feet over the bed. She gave me a glass of wine and a plate with some cold yellow porridge with cheese on it and she kissed me, and told me her name was Virginia. So I told her I was an officer off an English ship and that my name was Bruno, which I thought was near enough. Presently she took off all her clothes. She had a very beautiful body though I don't think she had had a bath for some time. So I took off my clothes and we made love and then I was afraid I should catch syphilis or something, and dressed and came away as fast as I could. She wanted me to stay the night, but I said I had to get back to my ship. I gave her a note of five thousand lire and I think she was surprised by it's being rather a lot. But she was terribly poor and I am glad I gave it to her. Then she called to a little girl playing in the yard and unlocked the door and the little girl led me all the way back to the harbour. And now you know all about it. She really was an awfully nice girl and that makes it a bit better.'

Billy listened to this description in silence, full of cold anger but avid for every detail.

'So that's what you are really like. Now I know,' she thought once or twice. After his last words her anger almost overcame her. He had taken his pleasure—directed she knew really against her—then he had thrown the girl

37

some money and had run away full of fear of the consequences for himself—but with no thought of what might happen to the girl: in a year or so another brat—David's child—might be crawling on the broad stairs of that slum tenement. David had never given a thought to that, and he was already trying to sentimentalize the affair and excuse his conduct because she was 'an awfully nice girl'. That seemed to her poisonous and she looked him in the face and said:

'I shan't ever ask you to make love to me again.' As she spoke she regretted her words. David had never looked more beautiful than with this serious, anxious look on his young face. His beauty hurt her. And the physical act of having washed his cock and having touched it, while it was fresh from another woman, made her feel as though she had somehow condoned his action.

But David had not apparently taken in the meaning of what she had said.

'You must tell me when it is safe for us,' he said. The insolent assumption that she would continue to want him was unforgiveable. But she was able to reply with no sign of emotion: 'Don't worry. I'm quite sure there's no risk. But now go and sleep by yourself for tonight and the next few nights. Then we'll see how each of us feels.' David went below. Billy sat in the cockpit. She did not need to touch the tiller—but watched the lights of the big boats coming in to Naples and the fishing boats sprinkled all around. She supposed that David was dreaming about Virginia. She sailed soon afterwards through the channel between Capri and point Campanetta. The sun rose as she

38

was just off Paestum and she steered in very close and caught sight of one of the temples through her binoculars. David was asleep and she did not wake him until she had made the coffee. After breakfast he took his turn in the cockpit and she undressed and got into her bunk. She was tired but she could not sleep for a long while and took a sleeping pill. She could not tell whether she was awake or asleep. But a train of thought that must have started in a dream continued and became more reasonable and logical and she became aware of the edge of the bunk—the plain wood against which her knee and her elbow had been pushed painfully. She had been dreaming, not that she was watching David with Virginia—though the girl was somewhere near—but that David had been watching her with someone else. But who? And as she became conscious, she thought of the men whom she had had as lovers and she knew that she had been silly—more than silly—wrong— to think so badly of David because of a casual encounter in the street. She remembered vividly, and with pleasure, a night when she had picked up a young sailor boy in Brazil. She had never told anyone about it—not even Sam —and she never would. The excitement and the touch of danger—she had taken him to a room in a cheap hotel used by prostitutes—was something she has never forgotten. And the sailor boy himself . . . How could she resent David's behaviour when she didn't even understand her own? 'But I do resent it. Hell it's too complicated. Let it slide,' she said to herself and dressed and went on deck. It was evening and there was land in sight.

They sat together in the dark, neither speaking. Billy

was not unfriendly, but as David didn't speak she was also silent. Suddenly he touched her arm and pointed.

'I think that there's a ship in distress over there.'

'I didn't notice anything,' said Billy.

'A rocket went up.'

They gazed silently for a long time while the *Connie* slid almost silently through the dark quiet sea, under a deep blue sky full of stars. Suddenly they both saw a streak of fire going up into the sky.

'That was no rocket,' said Billy.

'Well, what on earth was it?'

There was a longer interval and then again a fiery something shot up into the sky.

'I know. Stromboli,' said Billy.

'What's Stromboli?'

'It's a volcano. But I didn't know it was as active as all that.'

'Let's go close and have a look.'

But the wind dropped and dawn broke, before they were abreast of the island and passed near a dreadful scree of lava, pumice and what might have been sulphurous shale falling like a vast rubbish dump from the side of the mountain into the sea. The fiery ejaculations were not visible in the light of dawn. The wind rose with the sun and they sailed swiftly to the next island, Panarea, where the harbour was so shallow that Billy thought it safer to anchor off the stone jetty and go ashore in the dinghy.

The first of the fishing boats were unloading their night's catch at the covered fish market. Billy bought two big lampreys, brown and yellow spotted. They put them in the dinghy and went for a stroll. Tourists and summer visitors and many of the inhabitants were still asleep in their flat-roofed Arab houses, in front of which were big circular masonry columns supporting flimsy coverings of split bamboo or vine trellises to give shade. There were prickly pears and capers in flower, with marvellous violet stamens. They found a baker's shop and bought four huge round loaves, a bag of flour and some yeast and loaded with these made their way back.

Panarea was as far south as they could go, as if the winds were light or contrary, they might not get back in time for David's school opening.

Billy told herself that there was no danger of David's allowing himself to be picked up by a girl again. Neverthe-less the experience at Naples and the swarms of holiday boats in the gulf of Spezia, had made towns even more repellent than usual. Billy planned not to touch at any port unless they found themselves short of water. But fresh water was unobtainable in Panarea.

'The steamer from Sicily is not due till the day after tomorrow,' they were told, and it was some time before they understood that Panarea is a waterless island, depend-ent on the rainwater that runs off the flat roofs into deep cisterns, constructed centuries ago by the Saracens and that the coastal villas were supplied with water from a tanker, which brought water once a week from Sicily. However Billy thought that they would have enough to get them back as far as Ischia. As it happened, directly they had headed back to the North West, the wind freshened and the sirocco carried them at great speed up the coast of

Italy. Billy kept well out to sea and, except at night, when they sighted bands of light sweeping the horizon, they saw nothing of the land and only an occasional fishing boat or steamer, or an occasional aeroplane droning over-head.

They made love, took turns every morning at being towed behind the *Connie*, lay beside each other under an awning that Billy rigged up out of a sail, as the sun was too hot to be endurable.

But still Billy said nothing about Sam and at moments her silence troubled her. Behind her silence was the fear that if anything disturbed the idyllic moment, she would lose David. A dread of what the future would bring kept her from discussing it with David. This was out of charac-ter, as Billy was not a moral coward. But in this instance she concealed her cowardice from herself as 'a hatred of complications.' David never spoke of his own future, of school, or of examinations. Handling the *Connie* in a stiff breeze, rolling up the mainsail for a reef was sufficient task.

The wind had dropped to a gentle breeze and the sun was almost unendurably hot. They took turns in diving overboard and catching a towing bar—and then to save exertion, or heaving the *Connie* to, the one on board would set the winch going and the tow rope would be hauled in mechanically until the swimmer could let go of the bar with one hand and catch hold of the ladder and then, sometimes being given a hand by the one on board, climb out.

After Billy came out for the second time, David looked at her naked body and bent down and licked up one of the salt rivulets running down from her shoulder. Billy was surprised; she looked at him, and then led him to the rug they laid on the fore-deck in the shade of the mast.

'Come and make love to me,' but then, to her surprise, David completely lost all self control and began sobbing and sat crumpled, with knees up and his hands over his face.

'I can't, I can't, I can't bear your being so good to me and going on loving me. It's not just kindness is it? You do love me?' And sitting there, hunched up, he was so young, so tender, that Billy wondered how she could touch him and how live with him without hurting him. What could such a coarse creature as she was do to reassure and make happy, this sensitive God-like child?

She began kissing him, putting her arm round his shoulders and pulling him close, and then when David's sobbing stopped, he came in to her and in the passive ecstasy of complete happiness which followed, she was aware that he was feeling far more, and far more complicated emotions than she could cope with. And then they both fell asleep and the good little *Connie* sailed on to the North West.

Day succeeded day and as they crossed the gulf of Genoa more steamers showed up and Billy realized greater care was needed in keeping watch. As a rule David took the first watch and at midnight went down and roused Billy.

On what was to be their last night aboard, he clutched her, kissed her and they looked into each other's eyes. Though he had made love that afternoon he wanted her again.

43

'Duty first,' said Billy, pulled on her heavy sailcloth jumper and went up to settle herself beside the tiller. David was soon fast asleep.

The *Connie* was riding on an even keel moving gently forward under the motor. David ran on deck in his pyjamas. They were just rounding the sea-wall into the harbour of Monte Carlo. Billy was glad of his help to pick up moorings. After a six hour spell in the cockpit, sailing, steering and navigating single-handed, she seemed to be perfectly fresh. David would have inveigled her into love making, but she brushed him aside.

'We have a hell of a lot to do, packing up the *Connie* for an indefinite period, and then getting away ourselves before Felix, or anybody who knows me, gets hold of us. Luckily Monsieur Thomas will help by taking all the sails ashore. It's fatal to stow them away in the least damp, as they are bound to be after an all night cruise. And he will give the motor a thorough greasing.' Monsieur Thomas did not turn up. Billy drove off in a taxi to the garage where she had left her car and it was almost an hour before she was back.

'I had to telephone to Sam in London and explain things,' she said.

'Who's Sam?'

'Oh, haven't I told you? Sam's my husband. He's a wonderful person.'

'What had you got to explain?'

'Well, quite a lot really. But principally why I don't intend to return home until your school starts. I told him it was the twentieth of September. Was that right?'

'It's the twenty-second actually.'

It was news to David that Billy was going back to her husband and that she assumed that he was going back to school. He was uncertain whether to do so or not.

They went to lunch at a restaurant near the quay so as not to dirty the dishes they had washed up. Then all the afternoon was spent in waiting for Monsieur Thomas, who did not turn up till it was five o'clock. There was a long discussion between Billy and him about laying up the *Connie* for the winter, scraping her bottom and painting her.

When he had gone, Billy said that it was too late to drive any distance and went off leaving David not knowing what she was doing and feeling irritable. At any moment fat Felix or some of the people who had seen him get drunk and disgrace himself, might come along and attach themselves. They were sure to recognize Billy's car. Finally it grew dark and David's anxiety was partly dispelled, but he was in terror that Billy would have picked up some friends. It was a relief when she returned and said that she had booked a suite of rooms at the Hotel des Anglais in Menton.

Directly they arrived at that distinguished, luxurious and comfortable old hotel, David's unhappiness and irritation returned. Billy was preoccupied and did not notice what he was feeling as they went up with the porter in the lift. They had adjoining rooms with inter-communicating doors and a bathroom in common. Nothing could have been more comfortable, but thinking about it afterwards, she realized that to David it seemed to be a blatant advertisement of their relationship. It was dinnertime and

45

after they had had a wash and brush-up, Billy led the way to the lift and to the dining-room. David trailed along angrily behind, savagely noting the interested glances of the diners at four other tables, one couple of whom at least were English.

At last Billy took notice of his ill temper.

'Why are you sulking, David?'

'I'm not.'

'Well something's biting you. What is it?'

'Let's talk about it afterwards.'

Billy raised her eyebrows, started to say something but thought better of it.

David was a little mollified by her recognition that he was angry. However he ate in silence and looked at her with rage when she referred to the *Connie*. His bad temper was so evident that Billy and he attracted far more attention from their fellow diners than they would have done if David had been able to make easy conversation with his companion.

By the end of the meal, he had got Billy worried and she was racking her brains to think of what she could have done. As soon as they got into their room she turned to him and said: 'Darling. Please tell me what I have done wrong. I'm frightfully sorry if I've been stupid—but I wouldn't have annoyed you for the world. Please understand that it was absolutely unintentional.'

'Not so loud,' said David glaring at her fiercely.

'What do you mean?' asked Billy bewildered.

'I don't want everyone in the hotel to overhear what you are saying.'

46

'But there's nobody . . .'

'Walls have ears . . .'

'Nobody can possibly hear what we are saying—and what would it matter if they did?'

'I don't want everyone to know that I am your lover.'

Billy reflected that many men of her acquaintance would have been only too pleased at such an assumption being made. She paused, however, to consider what to say and David continued: 'I'm not a gigolo and I don't like to be mistaken for one.'

Billy burst out laughing.

'Darling glorious idiot. I may be a lot older than you but nobody looking at me would think that I had to pay my lovers to come to bed with me. If that is what you think, you are being just a wee bit insulting.'

'I wasn't thinking of it from your angle,' said David.

'Well if you do, you see it clears your character.'

'Anyway, I hate this damned place.'

'Well I'm going to take advantage of the bathroom and have a hot bath. Come and talk to me while I have it.'

'Somebody may come in.'

'Nobody will come in. Nobody cares a hoot about us as long as we are contented while we are here, and pay our bill when we leave. Actually they are awfully nice people.'

'Have you stayed here before with somebody else?' asked David suspiciously.

Billy laughed at him and, when she had had her bath, she stayed gossiping with him while he had his. They got into the big bed and Billy made love to him before she would let him come to her.

'I want to see you and kiss you and admire you. I want to take my time. Don't try and hurry over the whole thing.'

Afterwards David insisted on going to his own room.

'Why on earth, what is the matter?' Billy asked.

'I might not wake up in time. The waiter might find me with you.'

'Why shouldn't he? Anyway, he won't come until we ring for him to bring us breakfast in bed.'

'I don't want him to know.'

'I hope you're not ashamed of me,' said Billy and for the first time there was a touch of uneasiness in the laugh which accompanied her words.

David picked up a pillow and sloshed her over the head. When she recovered herself from the attack, he had gone. Billy overcame the impulse to jump out of bed and go after him.

'I'm being stupid. But I don't understand why he feels like this,' she said to herself. She turned the light out and before she had solved the puzzle, she was asleep.

When she woke in the morning it was all clear to her and she wondered why she had found it difficult to understand. Only, perhaps, because it was such a youthful emotion. The explanation, at which she had arrived, was that David was uneasy because he could not accept the situation in regard to society and his instinctive dislike of anything equivocal showed itself in a dislike of his surroundings. He was shy. Perhaps if she could make him face the fact that it was only shyness, he would get over it.

She got out of bed and went into the adjoining room.

David was already awake and reading a book. Billy sat on the bed and he pulled her head down and kissed her.

'Get in here.'

'Come to the big bed.' David shook his head and she climbed in, squashed beside him. He came into her at once and rode her furiously. When he had come he pushed her to get out of the bed and said: 'No, go back to your room and ring for the waiter to bring breakfast.'

Billy was feeling dazed, but she obeyed. After the waiter had gone, leaving their trays of coffee, croissants, butter and peach jam, she called gently to him:

'Bring your tray and have breakfast beside me.'

'No. I have got to leave crumbs in my bed.'

However after he had finished his breakfast, he came into her room and sat beside her.

'Why are you so shy?' asked Billy.

'I'm not shy. I hate people knowing anything about us. Our making love is private and secret and we can't keep it secret in a huge place like this.'

'What you are saying is shyness. You are just like a bride on her honeymoon.' David seized a pillow but before he could hit her with it, she said: 'Violence is no argument.'

'I won't have you calling me a bride.'

'Well, don't be so ridiculously shy.'

'I'm not shy. But I hate advertising our relationship. It's indecent.'

'Nobody bothers their heads about us here. They think we're quite ordinary,' said Billy.

'Well I don't want to stay in such a big place again.'

'Tonight we'll stay in a bistro with one room and three lorry drivers snoring in it. Then perhaps you won't think it indecent,' said Billy. David began laughing. Then he whispered: 'Would you mind if I got into bed with you again?'

Billy sighed luxuriously and stretched herself in the bed.

She stopped in Menton to buy food for their lunch, then drove through Nice and up into the hills away from the people and the sea. They sat down for their picnic and had spread out the food, when David stood up and began searching all his pockets.

'I've lost my lovely knife; the one that you gave me. I must have left it behind on the boat.' He was so upset that Billy handed him her own and said: 'Take this one instead. I'll buy myself another when we get to Paris, or somewhere.'

Then, as he hesitated, she insisted. 'Please take it. I want you to have it. Oddly enough a knife is the only thing that I've ever given you.'

David took the knife and then shook her and kissed her and said:

'I can think of a good many other things besides the lovely knives.'

Actually Billy did not buy herself another knife, for when she had the opportunity she forgot.

But the gift of the knife had set David thinking.

'You said it was insulting of me to suggest that I was

your gigolo. But though you say that you've never given me anything but a knife, you actually pay for everything, and you do it because I make love to you and repay you with pleasure.'

'Do you only make love to me because you want me to pay your share of the hotel bills?' asked Billy miserably.

'No, I don't and you know quite well that I don't. My love-making has nothing to do with money.'

'Well explain why you do?' said Billy fiercely. She hated explanations and analyses but as David seemed intent on one, she would have to face it.

'Love isn't just one's own pleasure, or giving pleasure. It's life itself: it's the wild excitement and thinking that one may really understand and, for a few moments become one, with another living creature.'

'You can have that complete intimacy without physical passion . . . but unless you have physical passion . . .' Billy was thinking of her husband, and did not finish what she had been about to say.

'Unless you have it what?' asked David.

'You said it was life itself. I suppose I agree. But it . . . it is not always even important. You and that girl in Naples . . .'

'Virginia was the only woman I've had, except you. I've not much to generalize on. But I would like to tell the truth. It was simple and good. If I hadn't been afraid of catching V.D., there was nothing wrong with it. She liked me and I liked her and afterwards we felt warm and loved each other and there was nothing cold or mercenary or wrong about it until I was suddenly frightened.'

Billy was silent and thinking to herself: 'Yes I can understand. Why do I hate his talking about Virginia, when I've been to bed with God knows how many men?'

'We couldn't speak to each other: only a few words. But we liked each other—loved each other for the moment and expressed our feelings with our bodies. It was only spoilt because I thought of possible consequences.'

'Consequences to yourself. She may be going to have a baby,' said Billy dourly.

'No I took care that shouldn't happen. I came out in time,' said David.

'I was unfair to you,' said Billy. David didn't seem to have taken in the implications of what she had said, and went on: 'Of course there's nothing like it. One is transported into Heaven: but it's not the pleasure. It's the sense of being alive—and then afterwards that sense of being new-born—like a snake that has sloughed its horny scales and is all brilliant colours and shining and tender.'

Billy caught him to her and kissed him. Then, when they had eaten and drunk and were lying in the shade of an ancient olive, propped up by its twisted trunk and roots, she went back to the subject of that morning.

'Your shyness worries me David. I want you to think about the whole subject dispassionately and to try to get over it. No. Please let me speak and don't interrupt indignantly until you have thought over what I am saying.' For David had begun to break in. He subsided and she continued:

'What you say is that our making love together is a private and secret matter. I agree with you. But it isn't only

52

because of our relationship—because you don't want to be thought my lover—that you are shy. It is because of the damnable English education which we all receive.'

'Excuse my interrupting. But I don't think it is anything to do with my education. It offends my taste to have people wondering about my intimate affairs—or rather to give them cause to wonder,' said David.

'That is just what I am complaining of,' said Billy. There was a pause.

'Go into any little French restaurant and you will find people who don't know each other talking and enjoying themselves. Go into an English equivalent and you find timid couples trying to get the tables next to the wall, or in a corner, and hoping that nobody will notice them. They talk to each other under their breath and speak as seldom as possible. What is the reason? It is because of the middle class damnable longing for gentility, and fear of saying something which will make people suspect that they don't "come out of the top drawer", sometimes not even that, but terror of being noticed at all.'

'Go on—finish what you are going to say,' said David.

'The French call it "*la morgue anglaise*" but it isn't *morgue*—it isn't arrogance, but shyness—only the French have no word for shyness in their language. The French word is *timide* but fear and shyness are completely different. *Pudeur* is really a better translation.'

'In my case it isn't fear of not being thought out of the top drawer—because, rightly or wrongly, I always assume that I am.'

'No, but your teachers don't believe that they are—and they pass on the middle class mentality,' said Billy.

'In my case it isn't shyness. Really it isn't. It is that it offends my taste to attract attention in places like restaurants and hotels. I think it is uncivilized.'

'Well darling. I've only seen you twice in a hotel or restaurant. The first time you got very drunk and quarrelsome and had to be carried home. The second time you drew everybody's attention to yourself by a most uncivilized display of bad temper.'

Suddenly Billy saw that David had begun to cry.

'Please forgive me being such a foul brute,' she said seizing him in her arms. He freed himself and got to his feet.

'Let's go on. I'll try not to be such an idiot again.'

Billy drove and David map-read for her, picking out very successfully the smallest little roads between the vineyards, which usually got them where they were aiming. They were driving slowly so as to look at a lovely old *mas* when David said:

'You don't mind everyone suspecting the truth, so long as you can hide it from one person.'

'What on earth do you mean?' asked Billy.

'I mean, for all you care, everyone can know we are lovers so long as Lord Tonson does not.'

'Lord Tonson? Do you mean Sam?'

'Yes, your husband. He mustn't know, though everyone

54

else may. I don't like that. It's not fair on him. It's treacherous . . .' Billy gazed at him with astonishment. 'I thought I told you that I had rung up Sam and explained it all to him.'

'Stop the car. I want to get this clear.' Billy pulled up. 'Do you mean that you told him that I was your lover?'

'Well, I made him understand.'

'So there will be a divorce. I don't mind. In fact it's wonderful. But you ought to have explained to me first, oughtn't you?'

'Oh God,' cried Billy wildly. 'Do listen and get this straight. Sam and I will never divorce each other. I love him and he loves me. But he is impotent. I can't explain it all now. And, by the way, Sam's not a lord. He's a knight: Sir Samuel. I thought you knew that.'

'Oh,' said David as it was borne in upon him that he was a fearful fool. But how was he to have guessed at anything so complex? And wasn't it, perhaps, worse for Sir Samuel for his wife to have lovers when he couldn't make love anyhow, than for her to be unfaithful in an ordinary way? That needed imagination and thinking out.

Half an hour later when they were driving again, Billy said:

'You must have been thinking I was the most awful God-damned bitch.'

'Well, I suppose I was beginning to wonder. I couldn't understand it,' said David.

'Well, I admit I seduced you darling. But I didn't do it in order to trap you into being a co-respondent at the age of seventeen.'

'Eighteen, actually,' said David.

'How's that?'

'To-day's my birthday.'

Billy stopped the car and kissed him. 'Many happy returns of the day. We must have a marvellous dinner with wonderful wine. I seduced you for quite different reasons. Or perhaps with no reason at all. Just because I was so madly happy that you were alive when I had nearly drowned you.'

'Well, I'll try not to be shy any more.'

'I have marked all the places where we have made love with a cross, on the map,' said David that evening during dinner. The English couple sitting behind him, overheard what he had said and stared. Billy actually felt herself blush.

Next day, however, David's shyness returned in an exasperating form. Without having explained why, Billy had, after Dijon, taken the route of the infant Seine. They had stopped for lunch at the Hotel Roy, Aisey sur Seine and, in the early afternoon, turned off into the byroads which led to the Château de Berri.

'There are some extraordinary people living in the Château here. I think they may ask us to stay for dinner, or put us up for the night.'

David was at once suspicious, and Billy had to describe St. Clair de Beaumont, a writer who had just achieved a success with a novel he had written in French, after writing several novels in English, which had attracted little attention. She explained also that his daughter, Alamein, was living there also with her husband, a young Italian inventor, and that St. Clair had a Russian mistress.

'They won't want us to drop in like this. I hate being unwanted,' said David.

'They'll love to see you. They are great friends of Sam's. St. Clair and his brother-in-law, Doctor Robert, were in the Resistance when he was. They'll be tremendously interested to meet you,' said Billy, tactlessly, as she drew up in front of the Château.

'I refuse to be exhibited as your lover. I shan't get out of the car,' said David stubbornly.

But already Alamein and her tall father, looking terribly spruce in a new suit of Glen Urquart tweeds, had emerged from the Château and were approaching.

'I won't get out,' repeated David.

'I shall be forced to tell them that you've got toothache,' said Billy in icy fury—and they were upon them.

'Why, it's Lady Billy! How lovely to see you!' cried Alamein.

'My dear lady, I was writing a little rondeau in the manner of Clément Marot to you, only yesterday,' drawled her father, bowing to kiss Billy's hand and then brushing up his moustaches.

'I'm sorry. I haven't come to pay a visit at all. I've come to ask for help in an emergency. This poor boy with me is in agony with toothache and I wondered if you could tell me of the nearest dentist.'

'We always go to Paris. I'll give you his address,' said Alamein, but she looked puzzled. 'I'll fetch some codeine, that might help.'

'Oh me poor boy, if you are really in *agony*, try *screaming*' drawled St. Clair. He was deeply concerned. 'Scream.

57

It's nature's cure for pain. There's nothing like it. Scream and scream and scream as loud as you possibly can.'

David didn't scream, but St. Clair de Beaumont had achieved a victory. David got out of the car and, holding a handkerchief to his cheek, shook hands.

'Any good psychologist will tell you that repression doubles the pain. So let yourself go. Don't feel shy or ashamed. We're used to it. At the first touch of pain, we all scream like peacocks.'

David held his handkerchief in front of his mouth. He had got the giggles. 'I'll go and scream in the wood,' he said in strangled tones.

'That's the thing. It's a marvellous cure. And now, dear lady, come in and Alamein will give you a cup of tea and I shall read you my rondeau. A very pretty little thing, as I'm sure you will agree.'

David ran off into the wood and screamed. They could hear him, even after Alamein had shut all the windows. It was a splendid performance and lasted a long time. After half an hour, he came and tapped at the French window.

'The pain has gone away,' he announced when he had been let in.

'Most gratifying,' drawled St. Clair. 'You are too late to hear my little rondeau. And I am afraid, Lady Billy, that you were too distressed, or too distracted by the noise your charming young Adonis was making, really to appreciate it. Never mind, I'll include it in my next volume of poems and shall dedicate it to you . . . You must *not* drink tea, my dear young man, or eat cake on any account or the pain will start again and, with lungs like yours, you will blow the roof off,' he added severely, for he had noticed that David was looking greedily at the tea table on which there was a cake with walnuts and almond icing.

'Well, do forgive us, we'll be getting on our way,' said Billy.

They left with the address of the Beaumonts' dentist and a bottle of codeine in Billy's bag. St. Clair stood beaming beside the little car.

'I am so delighted I was able to help your ever so beautiful boy-friend,' were his last words, but Billy noticed that Alamein was looking puzzled as she waved goodbye.

'Well, my ever so beautiful boy-friend, wasn't all the agony and all the shyness worth it?' asked Billy as they turned out of the drive.

'Did it sound all right?' asked David.

CHAPTER THREE

DIRECTLY they had reached Paris, Billy and David had run into the people they had taken pains to avoid in Monte Carlo. But now Billy seemed to be pleased to see them.

'I have made a considerable improvement on the classic method of serving dormice,' said Felix contentedly.

'What's that?' asked Billy.

'Well the flavour is good enough. In fact I think it is delicious, but the tiny bones are an infernal nuisance. So today I put half a dozen skinned and gutted *loirs*, edible dormice you know, with their heads removed too, into the electric mixer. I then added very thick honey from Rocamadour; it's a wild thyme and heather district, a little salt and pepper, put the paste in a tin and cooked it in a pressure cooker. After that I made enough paste to fill other tins. I filled the first as I said with plain *loir* and honey, a second with a little added pure butter and truffle, a third with honey and butter and truffle and a fourth with butter, honey and poppyseed. Will you all come tomorrow morning, to my first tastings?'

Next morning David said: 'I'm going off alone; I want to see some pictures while I'm in Paris.'

'Well, you've got Felix's address. You can pick me up there at the dormouse tasting about twelve.'

'I don't think I want to. I would rather explore a bit on my own.'

Billy knew that David didn't like Felix, but she wondered whether he also wanted to get away from her. It looked as though he did, but she was careful not to go into the matter.

'All right. I'll expect you when I see you.'

That evening Billy suggested that they should fly back to England the next day.

'You will want a few days in London and anyhow I want you to get to know Sam and to talk over your future with him.'

'I don't at all want to meet him,' said David.

'Don't be ridiculous. Anyhow you will be staying with us.'

There was finality in her voice and a hint of exasperation behind it. David was silent. He could not tell her that it was her own fault that he did not wish to meet her husband. If she had not told him that he was her lover; if she had not explained that her husband was impotent, it might have been possible. But with each knowing what he did about the other, David felt it was out of the question. But it was difficult to tackle Billy and he left it until a chauffeur in a peaked cap had seized hold of his suitcase when they had passed through the customs and was leading the way to a private car.

'Billy, do you mind dropping me on the way? I would rather stay at an hotel.'

'Don't be an owl,' said Billy pushing him ahead of her into the car. 'I shan't do anything of the kind,' she added as the chauffeur slammed the door and then got into the front seat.

Billy felt David boiling with indignation beside her and waited, expecting an explosion at any moment. He had only to lean forward and say to Jervis: 'Just pull up at the next lamp post—' and then get out. She would be helpless. She dared not touch him, dared not take him by the hand and plead with him. And his hatred for her filled the car like a mephitic gas. It paralyzed her. And as the explosion did not come, she began to have hopes that they would reach Belgrave Square and to feel guilty.

She knew it was always wrong to force anyone to do something against his will—and much more wrong if he were someone you loved.

And she knew that Sam, on whose account she was doing this, would tell her it was worse than wrong—it was mistaken and destructive of love. As the Bentley turned into Belgrave Square, she was on the point of calling out to Jervis, 'Stop here: Mr. Bruin wants to get out.' Should she speak? But meeting David's stony glance she realized it was too late. Then as they alighted, he said:

'If you insist on my meeting your husband, I should like to do so as soon as possible.'

'I expect Sam's still in bed. You had better wait till lunch.'

'I would much prefer to meet him straight away,' said David in a voice which trembled with passion.

'All right. I'll go and tell him.'

Billy went into Sam's bedroom. He was lying absolutely relaxed, propped up with a number of pillows in a bed which was a very gorgeous example of the French cabinet maker's art, with wreaths of flowers, swags of fruit and the amours of Zeus displayed in the enrichments of head and foot and with silver brocade hangings. Byelka, the Burmese cat, lay beside him, suckling two kittens.

His secretary who was taking dictation, rose and left the room as Billy went up and put her arms round Sam's neck and embraced him vigorously.

'Oh, darling. I'm longing to see you and tell you all about everything. And you are looking so well. Has Mrs. Harris been looking after you properly?'

Sam looked at her and Billy recognized the deep love in his eyes.

'Oh yes. Julia is very attentive and forsees all my needs and provides for all of them—except you. I've been wanting you so much—and I couldn't help being terrified of your drowning yourself in saving your schoolboy. Is he here by the way?'

'I've had to drag him here by the scruff of the neck. And he's outside and insists on seeing you immediately. He's terribly dignified and honourable and wants to bolt out of the house. I'm sorry, but will you see him straight-away?'

'Of course I will, if you want me to, darling.'

Billy went to the door and soon returned. She watched David go into the bedroom, holding himself very upright, stiff and yet at ease and she thanked God, not for the first time, for his good manners. As she shut the door it struck her that her lover had a good deal of moral courage for a boy just eighteen, and that he must be feeling that she was making great demands on him.

Well she would hear all about the interview from Sam, even if she didn't get much out of David. In this supposition she was mistaken. For a good hour later, David came to look for her with an expression that was joyous, even enthusiastic.

'He's an extraordinary man, Billy. I love him and admire him because he loves you so much. And I'll stay, of course, if you still want me to.'

Billy had felt confident that somehow Sam would bring this miracle about—but as she listened her mouth twitched and as she kissed David, she felt the tears coming. She took him to see his bedroom to cover up her emotion. David scarcely looked at it and said: 'He has such wonderful eyes. I shall never forget his look when he said you were such a rare creature and because we both loved you, we must never quarrel as that would hurt you too much. Oh, and we gave you entirely different things. I might have resented that and it might have made me jealous, if anyone else had said it. But I should be ashamed of feeling that, even though it implies I am nothing but the body and physical love—after meeting . . . Sir Samuel.'

'For Christ's sake call him Sam. But what did you say to him?' asked Billy. She did not want to embark on definitions of her love for Sam and her love for David.

'Oh, I want to forget that . . . I think I said that I had not wanted to come to his house, or to meet him, but that you had insisted on my doing so. Also that as I had no intention of giving you up, I had better go to a hotel until I went back to school. That is if I decided to go back.'

Sam was less communicative. Billy had to be content with:

'Oh he's so touchingly young and anxious to be honourable.' Billy who was anxious and earnest, saw that Sam didn't want to talk. And that was all that she could get out of him before she was shooed away in favour of a memorandum that he was writing in a hurry for the next meeting of the World Bank.

They were at dinner when Sam said: 'I think that we might have a party before David goes back to school—in fact we must have a party whether he goes back or not. And you must tell me what you think about that tomorrow. But we had better send out invitations tomorrow: let me have a list for my secretary of any friends you would like to invite David.'

David reflected. At last he said: 'There's Brian Milburne and then there's that girl Gundred something or other. I met her again in the Louvre and promised to look her up.' As he said this he caught the expression on Billy's face and he was suddenly inspired to say: 'She and Brian seem to know each other. Isn't that odd?' Billy smiled and drew a breath and said: 'Her name is Evans and she has a room in Benny Rumpelmayer's house.' Billy's moment of agony had passed, if it had ever existed. The ground was solid under her feet: a moment before and she was aware that there were abysses in the unknown.

'And all your usual crowd, I suppose Billy?' asked Sam.

'I suppose so,' said Billy without enthusiasm.

'Let me know if there's anyone you want to leave out,' said Sam.

'And who are your especial guests, Sir?' asked David.

'Don't call me Sir, David. My guests?' Sam meditated, but he was obviously pleased by the question. And he mentioned a few names famous in the world of music, literature and the theatre.

CHAPTER FOUR

ROMA PALGRAVE and Derek Hughes had come to lunch and Fat Felix had taken over Sam's suggestion of a party and had made it—not exactly his own—for Sam would pay and it would be in Sam's house, nevertheless everything would be carried out in accordance with Felix's ideas.

'I know just how . . . just what . . . just where to lay my hands on . . . just who will make it really a historic event . . .' In such a style he bubbled. And, as he bubbled, Billy could see that David glowered and looked with aversion at Fat Felix and at Derek Hughes. What was David feeling? How she hated all this. There was something ignoble in watching the person you loved, like a cat watching a mouse. When the lunch party had broken up, she went in search of Sam whom she found in a sunny little conservatory at the back of the house which he had transformed into a little workshop where he bound books, finding a complete rest from his business in delicate manual work.

'Come in Billy,' he said. She walked about restlessly not knowing how to begin and Sam went on: 'I got the impression that you weren't very happy at lunch.'

'I wasn't.'

'Well, what is the trouble?'

69

'All these complications ought to be swept away,' said Billy.

'Explain.'

'These complicated feelings and complicated situations: they are all unnecessary. People are much more simple than they pretend.'

Sam laughed. 'I don't agree Billy. I'm extremely complicated, you are complicated though you like to think that you are not. Your schoolboy is complicated and I think that you have already begun to find it out. Felix is probably more complicated than any of us—mind you I am not saying more interesting—but more complicated, because he doesn't like what he is, but can't do anything about it, whereas you and I do at least accept ourselves for what we are.'

'Talking of Felix—I don't think that your idea of a party was a good idea,' said Billy.

'Why not?'

'It's upsetting and it comes just when we three want to be at peace and to get to know each other better, before David goes back to school.'

'Did David say that he didn't like the idea of the party?'

'I haven't talked about it to him,' replied Billy. 'But he doesn't like Felix.'

'Well it was you who invited Felix—not me. And David seems quite eager to see his friend and that girl!' Billy changed the subject.

'I do so want you two really to get to know each other. I think that a man can talk to him about his future so much better than a woman.'

'I think that David and I know each other as well as we

are ever likely to,' said Sam. Billy looked at him in surprise. It was a cruel thing for him to say and she had never known Sam cruel. Could it mean that after all he didn't like David? But surely with someone as perceptive and sympathetic as Sam that would be impossible. Sam continued to be cruel.

'It's too late to call the party off. After all, you can't prevent the boy meeting girls of his own age. You must reconcile yourself to that my dear.' What was so bloody about Sam was that he could put into words what one wouldn't admit to oneself. Billy's eyes smarted as she held back tears. And Sam stood up and placing the book he had been patiently sewing between two boards, inserted it carefully in the press.

Billy knew that he didn't want to say anything more and went away miserably in search of David. But he had gone out without telling her, or saying where he was going.

Sam was probably right and he had gone off to see a girl of his own age. Billy thought she wouldn't have minded if there hadn't been such a terribly short time before he went back to school, in which they could do things together. And she had to organize that damned party.

But the party didn't take place. When David woke up next morning he found that it was later than usual and that Sally, the maid, had not brought him early morning tea, an omission for which he was thankful, as he only drank a cup so that her trouble in climbing up to the third floor should not have been wasted.

Downstairs he drank a cup of coffee and ate a kipper and then Billy came in with her arms full of parcels.

'You've heard? Sam's had a heart attack. He's better now. We have got a nurse to look after him.'

David looked scared and Billy went on: 'I haven't any colour prejudice—don't mind negroes and Indians—but I couldn't help blinking when a bright yellow banana made her appearance—with hair like a brass wire saucepan cleaner. When she went out of the room Sam asked me if he had jaundice—quite seriously. He thought he was seeing things. I must go and rescue him from her.' Billy laughed and was hurrying from the room, when David asked: 'Hadn't I better go away?'

'Please, please don't do that. You may be able to help me. The party's cancelled of course. It would help if you keep yourself amused today.'

'Is there any danger?'

'He responded to the drug. The doctor thinks he's all right. But he will have to keep very quiet for a fortnight and lay off work.' Sam wasn't well enough for David to see him before he went back to school the next morning. Billy drove him to Waterloo with all his bags and boxes.

'I'll write and tell you how Sam goes on and we'll spend your half term together,' said Billy and kissed him in front of a crowd of schoolfellows and the mathematics master. David put his hands on each side of her face and kissed her back on the mouth.

Half term was early in November and Billy drove down to Dorset to carry David off for four days. The sky was clear for most of the day and though the sun was hot, the air was cold. She drove into the grounds of the eighteenth-century palace which had been turned into a Public School and parked her car. Though many of the elms had shed their leaves, a few still kept patches of torn green foliage. But the beeches were magnificent: the leaves were drifting down, but they were still thick enough to cast a shade over the dull red-brown carpet beneath them. But in the sunlight the beech leaves shone orange and red. Billy walked out from the shadow and stood for a little, looking at the beauty of the palace, which was at the same time severe and civilized. Its grandeur was absolutely free from arrogance and she wondered if the Dukes who had lived in it had achieved as good manners as their home.

Groups of boys and parents were clustering round the steps which led to the main entrance.

David, who was on the lookout, suddenly recognized her figure and a wave of eager happy excitement came over him. She was so tall, so thin, so handsome, so entirely unselfconscious. He ran down the stairs and across the forbidden lawn, reserved on ordinary days for the head master and his guests, and seized her by both hands and stood for a moment holding her and gazing at her.

'What is it, David?'

'You are so beautiful I don't believe you are real.'

Billy laughed happily.

'Have you got your car there? Let's get away. I've hidden my bag by the lodge gates.'

'All right. But I would like to see your study and the building.'

'You can do all that when you bring me back.'

They walked back to the car and drove off. At the lodge Billy pulled up and David jumped out and pulled out his bag from behind a rhododendron bush.

'Turn right up this next by-lane,' said David.

Billy looked at him enquiringly. 'It's not on our road.'

'Do what I say.'

She turned up it.

'Another hundred yards. Round that corner . . . That will do.' Billy pulled up. 'Now kiss me, you cold blooded woman. Did you think I would wait until you had driven a couple of hundred miles?'

This was a new, older David who gave orders and took the initiative in love making.

Three hours later Billy's two seater was bumping along a cart track in thick fog and David had often to get out and walk ahead to make sure that there was a track at all. They were in a wood.

'Here's the pillar box you were talking about,' he said.

'Now I know I'm right. It's about two hundred yards to the left through a wood. Lead on.'

The headlights lit up a blur, which was paler than anything they had come upon before. It was a clearing among the trees. Billy drove slowly into it. On the far side was a dark object: a hut. She turned so that the headlights shone on the door. Then she got out and unlocked it. A moment later she had switched on the lights and yellow bars shone out of the windows. Now that they had arrived and were alone, David seemed to have forgotten the urgency of making love. He walked round and round the room scrutinizing everything.

'You're like a cat in a new house.'

'What is this place you've brought me to?'

'It's a fishing lodge. We're in Wales.'

'I know that. How did you get hold of it?'

'Borrowed it from my brother. It practically belongs to him. It is on the Treforest estate. Lord T. is only five and my brother is his agent. In another month the salmon fishing will have started and I couldn't have got it.'

The wind was blowing, spatters of rain and falling leaves struck wet on their faces as they unloaded the car and carried in bags, bundles of blankets and boxes of provisions. The wind whirled through the open door and David blinked in the light. It felt adventurous, piratical; and the boy remembered that moment of arrival long afterwards as one of complete happiness. When the last armful had been brought in and the door shut, there was sudden quiet and Billy and he looked at each other, silently wondering: 'What is it going to be like? What lies in store for me?'

Their new home was a big wooden hut with a calor gas cooker and a stove burning wood for heating.

Billy found a packet of firelighters and while she was unpacking and putting the provisions away in the cupboard, David lit the stove. A puff of wind blew down the chimney pipe and smoke billowed back into the room.

He coughed, found a newspaper, held it in front of the stove and it drew. No more smoke came. By the time he was satisfied, Billy had laid out plates and cut slices from a ham, and opened a bottle of beer. David came and sat in silence, Billy helped him and they ate, looking up at each other and grinning between the mouthfulls.

At each end of the hut was a bunk tucked away high up in the roof, reached by a gleaming metal ladder. David climbed up one of these, but announced that two people could not sleep safely in one bunk—then pitched down the mattress, later climbing the other ladder and throwing down the second. Billy and he put them together in one corner of the room and then made up a bed on the floor. Then they undressed and went to bed, leaving the task of washing up until the morning.

Love making was brief, for David was over eager and both of them were tired. Billy indeed realised that she was very, very tired, as she lay awake after David had fallen asleep. She stared open-eyed into the darkness, seeing the vague outlines of the table and the chairs which she knew were there. At last she fell asleep but for some reason woke up a few hours later. Moonlight fell in a narrow bar from the window. She drew herself cautiously out of the bed on to the floor, then got on to her feet and putting on an over-coat stepped out into the brightly lit night outside.

Rain was over; clouds were gone; the moon three-quarters full, rode high up and the black bars of the trees cast waving shadows. She squatted among the leaves, an owl hooted and she felt suddenly as fierce and as much alive as the owl:—as wild as the nightbird, as unafraid and also deeply content to be herself. The wind blew and chilled her but she lingered happily, staring at the moon through the trees with her hand on the latch.

76

The owl hooted again, she opened the hut door, stole in and slipped gently beside her sleeping lover.

It was nine o'clock; she had the fire lit and the coffee machine bubbling, before David opened his eyes.

'Come back here,' he said.

'Get up you lazy lout.' Billy gave him a gentle kick but he caught her leg and tried to drag her down. She hit him and escaped.

'I want to get out with a gun. There are pheasants around.'

There were coffee, eggs and bacon, toast and marmalade. Then clearing up the hut and washing up and getting out the guns and putting on boots took almost an hour, and it was near eleven before they went out. David was armed with an old hammerless non-ejector by Holland and Holland, Billy with her lightweight Churchill XXV.

'That gun you are shooting with is a work of art. Feel the balance of it! I am so used to shooting with short barrels and my gun has been fitted to me—that I could not change. But sometimes, when I lift your gun, I feel tempted to.'

'Whose is it?' asked David.

'It belonged to my elder brother who was killed in nineteen forty. And it was an old gun before he ever had it.'

'I shall never hit anything,' said David. 'I've never fired a shotgun. I'm not too bad with a rifle.'

'Forget the rifle. When you see a bird, fling up the gun, swing it and fire while you swing.'

They went out into the wet woods and followed a path

77

where moles had been at work, which led to where a narrow meadow divided the woodland.

'Stand here. I shall work my way round and beat through. If a bird breaks cover, swing at it and fire—and don't forget that you have a second barrel which may bring it down.'

Billy left him and crept back silently to the far end of the wood. When she had got into it, she found that the undergrowth was very thick and tangled and that twigs were always whipping her face and catching her gun barrels. It was impossible to see more than ten yards. As she hesitated, she saw a rabbit only a few yards away. She did not want the rabbit, yet she could not restrain herself from raising her gun. But before she could fire, the rabbit hopped behind the bole of a beech and next moment two pheasants flew up, almost vertically between the ash poles. Billy swung her gun instinctively and fired though she had actually lost sight of the pheasant at that moment. The bird fell, a fine cock, and Billy retrieved him lying stone-dead in a patch of brambles. As she picked him up, she heard a shot from David. That would be the other bird flying out of the wood to the next coppice. Billy pushed the cock pheasant into her game bag and cautiously went on.

A pheasant rose from a little behind her, where it had been crouching and she spun round, firing as she spun and it plunged precipitately to earth. Stone-dead, but this time a hen. When Billy had got to the edge of the wood, she could see David waiting with the gun in his hands, though he had not seen her. Two pheasants, which had been crouching in the ditch, rose with a tremendous clatter.

David fired first at one bird and then at the other and missed each of them. While he was reloading, a cock pheasant sprang into the air directly between Billy and David. She could not fire because of David and he was caught with his gun open, reloading, and the cock sped away like a glorious comet.

Billy struggled out of the wood, unaware that her face, whipped by a briar was bleeding profusely.

As she emerged she saw that David was holding up a hen pheasant and she was at once bursting with delight and relief. He had shot it with his first shot.

'Magnificent. How splendid of you,' she exclaimed.

'What have you done to yourself?' he asked, and it was only then that Billy realized that blood was running down the side of her nose into her mouth, and that there were torn off thorns stuck in her eyebrow and cheek and at the side of one nostril.

'Splendid of you to have got that bird with your first shot.'

David told her to stand still and mopped the blood with his handkerchief and then, as she stood motionless, holding her face up to him, he pulled out the bits of rose thorn with his nails. The pain and the blood were blessed, because David was touching her. She swallowed and the taste of her own blood was good. She was glowing with happiness.

'Can we cook it for supper tonight?' asked David stroking his bird.

'We can't. A pheasant has to hang ten days at least. You have the glory, but I shall have the pleasure of eating it. And Sam and I will drink your health when we eat it.'

Promise to tell Sam that I shot it.'

'Of course, you oaf. And my chief boast will be that I taught you how to shoot . . . just as I have taught you how to do other things.'

'Do you boast of that too?'

'I ought to.'

'Just look at the feathers on the head,' said David stroking them.

Billy and David were happy all through the four days of the half-term holiday. Trouble came on the Sunday evening as they came in the early darkness to the school.

'Drop me by the park gate,' said David.

'You promised you were going to show me your room,' said Billy.

'O.K.'

She was aware that she had said the wrong thing as she drove along the winding private road between the trees and aware that David had grown withdrawn and tense with embarrassment. But it was too late to turn back.

'Well, come on up.'

She picked up one of his bags and followed him as he led the way into a great empty hall from which a superb double staircase sprang.

'What a marvellous staircase.'

'Everyone says that. It's supposed to be the best of its kind in England.'

David led the way down a corridor, then up a small staircase into the attics and opened his study door. It was a small room with a table, a desk and a single bed. And pinned on the wall was a half length charcoal drawing, life size, of a young man stripped to the waist. Billy instantly recognized it. It was David. She stared at it for some moments, noticed that it was initialled G.E. in the bottom corner. But she said nothing.

David had forgotten the drawing was there, and even if he had remembered, its presence would not have seemed important to him. Now he realized that it might be.

'Have some tea.'

'No. I must go now.' Billy was shivering violently. David wanted her to go, but the shivering alarmed him, so he caught hold of Billy's arm.

'Now you have come, you must stay,' he said and drew her stiff unyielding body towards him. At that moment the door was flung open, a fair haired boy precipitated himself into the room, pulled up short and exclaiming 'Sorry,' backed out hastily.

Billy disengaged herself.

'Goodbye David.'

'I'll come to the car with you,' cried David and ran after her. Billy said nothing until she had settled herself in the car, and put on her gloves. Then she pulled herself together and smiled at him.

'Thank you darling for a lovely holiday,' she said. Then let in the clutch and disappeared into the darkness—only the red lights of the tail lamps curling away, disappearing and reappearing among the trees.

'Oh, why, why am I so silly? I shall spoil everything,' she exclaimed.

When she had driven a few miles, she stopped the car to find a handkerchief and then drive on.

CHAPTER FIVE

ON TWELFTH NIGHT they had the party, which had been postponed because of Sam's sudden illness in October.

It was in three parts: a concert of Elizabethan and Restoration songs to an accompaniment of guitar, followed by Spanish songs with the same instrument, providing a fascinating contrast of mood and feeling. Then came the dinner, the menu of which had been drawn up and many of the dishes prepared by Felix Hotchkiss, after which there was dancing to a small band led by a world-famous trumpeter. The mixtures were too violent for the party to be wholly a success. Late arrivals kept breaking in upon the concert and as they creaked into the room looked thoroughly bewildered, for they had not expected the delicacies of Dowland.

Then Felix's discoveries in the way of food alarmed many of the guests, who seemed to suspect that a practical joke was being played at their expense.

Snails with garlic? Sea Urchins with pepper sauce? Frogs' legs in aspic? Dormice in honey? Roast thrush? Wild Boar with whortleberry sauce? Badger's ham? Pankak's Torta? What could one choose out of such an assortment? Even the drinks were as dangerous and alarming as the food. Bucelas! Resinato! Raki! Saki! And the long haired and bearded flower child, who asked for a soft drink, was given the choice of Kéfir, or hot sweet mint tea.

The young people held out their plates for second helpings of badger or dormouse and filled their glasses with bucelas—but the enthusiasm sometimes curdled into horror: Roumanian *mittardi* sausages and cold rice were shovelled aside untouched, unfinished glasses of resinato were poured into pots of arum lilies, to be refilled with whisky or champagne.

But already in the next room they were dancing to a very noisy band presided over by Jaimé. But the really terrific noise inspired curiously little movement among the dancers. The young girls with rapt expressionless faces, the young men looking rather dutiful, bobbed up and down, turned sideways, pressed their bodies together and moved apart like a crowd of tadpoles in a glass bowl, standing on their tails and shooting up to the surface of the water with quick shivers running through their tails. Yes. They were pairs of wriggling tadpoles.

Billy tried her hand at dancing with David, but he could not let himself go to the music. She guessed that to be seen dancing with her, revolted him. She was tall, she was angular, she was awkward, she was old. Almost the oldest woman in the room. And from the way he looked at her, anyone must be able to see that he was feeling ashamed of her. All his early shyness and surliness had returned. He did not want people to guess that they were lovers. But stuck there, among the tadpoles in the bowl, she could not get away and immediately the band stopped, it started again and they were trapped for a while. At last there was a longer pause and she disengaged herself and without saying anything, went into the next room. When she came back he was dancing with a girl she hadn't seen before and talking eagerly to her. Gundred had brought a young man called Ronnie. Billy thought he was like a small well-polished black shoe. His hair black, his face white with one or two spots and eyes that revealed nothing, they were like plums with those patches of brown rot on them that come in a wet summer before the fruit is ripe. Perhaps he was stoned with pills, or hashish. Sam had gone to bed, but the dancing went on. At last it stopped and Gundred and Ronnie and David and the girl in scarlet went up to each other.

'Hullo David. You two know each other don't you? I love dancing with Ronnie. He becomes part of my body. You wouldn't be any good. But come and look at the loan collection in the National Gallery tomorrow. You are good at looking at pictures.' Her voice rang out so loud that Billy was not the only one to catch the sudden eager change in David at her last words, and to see him nod acceptance. And then the girl's voice rang out again to proclaim: 'If Ronnie's my body, I suppose you are my eyes: twin inlets of soul the poet called them—was it Donne? I'll wait inside the turnstile at three o'clock. Mind you are there when I arrive.'

David went to bed before the last of the party had gone, Billy had to wait to the very end. She did not go to David's room. She could not, after seeing that look of surprise and anger, and then, the sudden transformation following Gundred's invitation.

85

But what did it mean? How far had it gone? At all costs she must find out. She could not live, if she were kept in doubt. And the fear came also that these young people took drugs and would ruin David. She got out of bed and took some drugs herself in order to deaden the pain, even if she couldn't sleep.

Billy had seldom been to an exhibition of pictures alone and of her own free will, and she had not been into the National Gallery since she was a girl at school. She felt ill at ease as she climbed the steps and reluctant to leave the pigeons and fountains of Trafalgar Square, but she was being pushed against her conscious will through the swing doors and then, feeling as though she were acting a part, walked up the staircase facing her. The great room in front was almost empty and she turned away instinctively from it. Looking back she noticed that most of the visitors to the gallery had turned in a steady stream to the left, so she retraced her steps and followed the crowd only to be pulled short to wait her turn at a turnstile. It was seven and sixpence to go in and ten shillings for a catalogue. 'I thought it was free,' she murmured but the ticket seller caught her words.

'The Krusoe loan exhibition.'

Of course. Krusoe was the name she had overheard Gundred speak of. Billy paid her three half-crowns and at the next table bought a catalogue. She had better read the introduction and learn what it was all about.

86

Without looking at any of the pictures, she walked right through into the end room, found a seat on the central settee and began to read. She learned that Mr. Krusoe was an American millionaire who had competed over many years with his brother (also a millionaire) in collecting pictures. Their jealousy, it was hinted, had been intense and their warfare profitable to the dealers. Fine as was the collection being shown in London, it was in many respects outclassed by the fraternal collection permanently housed in New England.

Billy was amused by this and was saying to herself: 'I think I'll go now I've found out what it's all about,' when she raised her eyes and saw David and Gundred standing within a few yards of her with their backs turned, looking at a picture. Fortunately she was a good deal hidden by the press of other spectators and she felt sure that they had not seen her. So long as their backs were towards her she watched them as best she could through the intervening jungle of heads, bodies and legs. They stared at the picture for such a long time that Billy began to think that there must be a reason for their behaviour. They did not speak to each other, or hold hands, but just stood and stared. Occasionally one of them moved impatiently, so as to see the picture better if someone got in the way. For some obscure reason, that picture seemed to mean a great deal to them. Finally Gundred moved to the next picture away from her, and soon afterwards David followed her.

Seeing them together a feeling of dread, of helplessness, of despair came over Billy. But what made her sensations so horrible was that they appeared to belong to somebody else. It was no longer the Billy whom she knew, who was sitting in the room. It was someone whom she had never known existed—an abysmal person. 'This isn't me. How did I get into this situation?' flashed for a moment across her mind. This creature, whom she had become, had torn the big illustrated catalogue nearly in two and then held up the fragments to hide her face, lest David should turn round and recognize her. But her hands were shaking and half the catalogue fell on the floor. With a great effort she bent down and picked it up. David's black head was close to the door; Gundred was hidden behind other people. Then, to her astonishment, she saw both of them pushing their way back through the crowd towards her. They were talking, for she could see Gundred laugh and turn towards David. She held up the torn catalogue again and, when two or three seconds later she lowered it, she could see that they were looking once again at the same picture, which had occupied so much of their attention before. However their scrutiny did not last so long the second time and soon they had joined the throng surging in and out through the door and they were gone.

Billy sat immobile for twenty minutes. Then, narrowing her long-sighted eyes she was able to read the number one hundred and forty seven pasted on the wall beside the picture. With her shaking fingers she turned over the pages of the torn catalogue until she found: Number one hundred and forty seven. 'Oh Matisse. Sam has one in his bedroom.'

Then she got up quickly and left the building. She had not looked at a single one of the exhibits.

While she had been sitting, waiting in the National Gallery, it had occurred to her that she might wake up suddenly and discover that the trance of horror and fear was over, and that it was not true that David no longer loved her. But while she stood waiting for a bus, she knew that even if the horrible trance-like feeling left her, an agony would be left behind. Nothing was going to be any good any more. She went home and only when she had put her key in the lock and opened the front door, did it occur to her that she would be meeting David in an hour or two. What could she say to him? How appear to be the woman she no longer was? David might even be in the house already.

'He hasn't seen me and I must forget this afternoon,' she said to herself. But it was impossible to forget an experience which had changed her into someone else.

David was not in the house and did not reappear. She had dinner alone with Sam, but did not say anything about having gone to the National Gallery and, though she thought he must have noticed that something was the matter, he was kind enough not to ask any questions and went to bed early.

David still did not come back and Billy sat up all night waiting for him. At half past six she decided to go to bed, undressed and took two sleeping pills. They had no effect and at half past eight hearing Sam moving in the next room, she got up and went into his bedroom.

He took one look at her and throwing open the bedclothes said: 'Come in here, darling.'

Billy sat down on the edge of the bed and said: 'I am

going mad. And I know now that I deserve to go mad. I'm a wicked, poisonous creature.'

'Come in here, darling and we'll talk about it.'

Billy knew that if she got into bed beside Sam, she might burst into tears and she wanted to be calm, to tell him what she had been thinking, to denounce herself to him.

But Sam took hold of her wrist and pulled her down and she allowed herself to be wrapped in his arms and then to be made to lie close to his long soft warm body, while the bedclothes were pulled up again around them. He kissed her mouth and stroked her forehead and brushed back her tangled hair and she burst into a storm of tears. Sam did not ask whether David had gone. He knew without asking and Billy was surprised again, as she was so constantly being surprised by his intuition, when he said:

'So you have been sitting up all night waiting for him. You had better get some sleep.'

'I've taken two pills. But they don't work.'

Billy had half expected Sam to console her by saying that all sorts of things might have prevented David coming home that night and that it was absurd of her to believe that he had left her. She would have found such reasonable forms of consolation unbearable, but Sam did not make them. He just held her close and stroked her forehead and kissed her occasionally. Billy swallowed back her tears and said:

'I'm in a turmoil, Sam. I've only just seen myself as I am. Nobody can ever love a creature like me. Even you couldn't, if you could see inside me.'

90

Sam said nothing, but went on stroking her hair and holding her tight.

'You see I'm guilty. I'm horribly guilty. I prey on you and now I debauch a child and run mad with jealousy because he likes looking at paintings with a girl his own age. I went there and spied on them. It was horrible. I was like an evil spirit in hell. Now that I have found out the truth about myself, I shall never be happy again. Even if it turns out that he simply got drunk last night. Even if he comes back to me.'

Sam went on stroking her head and under his gentle caresses she began to feel calmer. The words: 'Nothing matters. Death comes to us all,' came into her head and seemed infinitely consoling. Then Sam was saying:

'Darling you must learn to accept whatever comes. Most things in life bring happiness. Some things hurt almost unbearably. But none of us are guilty. I am what I am. You are what you are. You must accept yourself and not torture yourself. Don't talk nonsense about being guilty and debauching David. You were wonderful to him and he will always love you and be grateful to you. Now sleep.'

How long Sam's quiet voice went on she did not know, for she presently fell into a dreamless sleep.

It was late in the morning and Billy stared about her, bewildered for a moment at finding herself lying alone in Sam's bed, before she remembered how she came to be there—and the sick realization that she had lost David came with it. She got up, went to her room feeling numb, had a bath and dressed. It was past mid-day. Sam was in the library, fully dressed, with his secretary, dictating. As soon as Billy opened the door he looked up and she heard him say:

'That's all for the moment, Julia. I'll give you the rest of it after lunch.' Billy knew well enough that he hated doing any work after lunch. He got up and went to meet her and taking hold of her hands drew her in and, looking at his face, she knew that he had something to say to her. She sat down and Sam went back and sat down where he had been, on the other side of the table.

'Has anything happened?' she asked.

'Yes, David came to fetch his bag while you were asleep. He asked to see me and said that he did not want to see you. But he asked me to tell you that he would always love you and feel grateful to you, but he thought it would be better for him to keep away because he knew that you felt too much for him and that he could not respond. I asked when he had seen you last and he said sitting in the National Gallery in the Krusoe loan collection, watching him. He did not speak to you or you to him, but it was then that he realized that you felt more than he did and he felt frightened of what might happen if it went on.'

'Oh my God. So he saw me after all,' said Billy. She could not avoid an angry note coming into her voice. 'Did he actually say he was *frightened*? Did he use that word?'

'Yes, darling, he did. And you must accept it.'

Billy was silent and after a pause Sam said quietly:

'Of course he'll come back.'

'Why on earth do you say that? Is it to try to console me, or hide the truth or what?'

92

'No. It's because I am quite sure it is true. Your relationship with David is only just starting.'

'But I'm forty-seven and he's only eighteen.'

'Age isn't important in this case and won't be for at least another five years.'

'You can't understand. I'm sorry Sam . . . But you just can't understand.'

'Nonsense Billy. I can see it all much clearer than you. This separation is really not important. It's probably necessary to you both.'

'If it weren't that I have a duty to you Sam, I should poison myself.'

'That's a beastly thing to say, darling. But I know you don't mean either part of the proposition. You know quite well that you have no duty to me—and you are far too sane and healthy an animal to poison yourself.' Sam got up, walked round the table and began to stroke Billy's head.

'Promise me you'll accept life. Promise.'

Billy sat motionless. She was feeling numb. She was feeling nothing at all. How odd to feel nothing! To be quite empty.

Then as she saw that Sam was waiting for an answer, she said: 'Oh—all right. I promise. I won't do anything stupid.'

'Come along. I'll mix you a drink before lunch. I feel I want one myself.'

Sam seldom drank before lunch and Billy knew that he was more upset than showed. Her life was over.

CHAPTER SIX

BILLY felt that her life was over: but it had to go on, and
to continue in a setting from which she always tried to
escape. She felt aggrieved, because Sam began making unusual demands on her at a time when she was miserably
unhappy, and she did not at all suspect that it was precisely
because she was so unhappy that he was seeking to distract
her by making them. Billy believed that she repaid Sam
for letting her go off sailing alone for months at a time, by
behaving like a model hostess when she was actually living
with him.

But she resented the fact that after David's departure,
Sam gave her little opportunity to be alone and that his
demands increased. He arranged dinner parties to be given
to Swiss and American bankers and their wives. Billy had
to entertain suspicious economists from Universities—men
whom Sam was anxious to soothe and flatter. Then there
were technologists, who had to be briefed on how to talk
to politicians, in order to make them realize what was not
only possible, but essential. There were Trades Union
Leaders to be inspired with uneasiness and to be tempted
by the ideas Galbraith had put forward of incomes for all,
and lives of guaranteed idleness.

It was beastly of Sam to take for granted that she would

play a part on all these occasions and even more beastly of him to accept invitations for her, as well as for himself, which it was impossible for her to get out of without having a row. And Billy had never felt less like having one. She did not guess, until weeks afterwards, that Sam was forcing her to take part in all these trivialities in order to give her less time to brood and mope.

He certainly forced her into a very different world from that of Felix and Roma and Billy's friends—and also from Sam's friends among painters, actors and musicians.

The talk with these economists and bankers could not interest her; with the men it was concerned with such things as bank rates, an international currency, a floating dollar or a creeping pound. Sometimes these discussions grew fierce, but Sam was never ruffled and was usually at his gentlest when pushed in argument. But he could be intentionally rude. Once when he realized that one of the leading gnomes of Zurich was not even trying to understand the subject under discussion, he smilingly remarked to the company: 'We must excuse Herr Stumpfel. He has lived all his life in the narrow Swiss valleys: we cannot expect him to have wide horizons. You remember the Victorian song: "Funiculi Funicula." Mein Herr has never paid his five francs to go up the funicular railway to look at the view.'

When his victim tried to interrupt, Sam waved him aside with: 'I am quite serious. The International Monetary Fund ought to buy a season ticket for him to the top of the Matterhorn. Herr Stumpfel has a pair of eyes in his head, but he has never had the opportunity to use them to look at the real world: he has been too busy deciphering balance sheets, but the real world is not contained in a balance sheet. The trouble is that there are lots of bankers and economists and Chancellors just like Herr Stumpfel. We have either got to make them open their eyes, or take away their jobs. That of course means revolution. Five francs up the funicular railway is a cheap alternative.'

There was uneasy laughter round the table and as the Swiss tried to open his mouth, Sam began singing: 'Funiculi, funicula.'

With the bankers' wives, Billy talked of hotels and holidays on the Côte d'Azur and towns along the coasts of Italy. All of them had been there and were eager to return to something just the same, but different in name, from where they had spent their holidays before. So Billy gave them tips: the names of hotels in places where she would never stay herself. The men, she thought, however dull, were better than their wives, and she reflected that it was curious that it was not true of all classes. Among British politicians, the wives were greatly superior to the husbands.

After one dinner party, Billy told Sam that she was sure the distinguished economist she had been talking to, took drugs. Sam asked her why she thought so.

'He has no flesh on his bones and his eyes glitter and he can't lift his glass to his lips without spilling.'

Sam shook his head and said: 'Hereward is a power-addict. He used once to have some power, but it has been withdrawn and he is wasting away for lack of it. For some people power is a drug, like heroin.'

'You have power Sam. How can you tell you are not an addict?'

'I haven't got very much power. But I may be an addict, or becoming one. I'm like our alcoholic friends who don't know that they are, until they find themselves somewhere where whisky is unobtainable.'

'Suppose you suddenly lost all your money, Sam?'

'Sangorski would take me on as a highly paid craftsman bookbinder, or I might start up a little business of my own.' It was clear to Billy that Sam had thought it out and would not feel his life was wrecked if he did lose all his money.

January and February seemed endless. Then one day, early in March, when she went into Sam's bedroom she caught a quizzical look on his face and heard him say:

'Too many tricks make a dull dog. You've done your whack most nobly. Isn't it time you took a holiday away from me, my dear? What about that new suit of sails you ordered for the *Connie*?' Billy stared.

'I mean it. There'll be sun down there. I can't come anyway, because of the fuss about the budget.'

Billy accepted Sam's proposal. When she and David had returned to England she had left her car in Paris, but Felix had driven it back to Nice for her. So she flew out to Nice, picked up her car and, the same evening, was looking at the *Connie* lying beside the quay at Monte Carlo. There was the little ship gleaming with paint and varnish, with her snow-white nylon rigging. There was the dirty water of the harbour and the line of the clean sea out beyond. There were the familiar smells. But for some reason that she did not understand, Billy's voice trembled and almost broke as she spoke to Monsieur Thomas and thanked him.

Yes, she would go on board that evening. Everything she had ordered was ready and had been put on board. She followed him into the little room like a cave, facing the quay, which served him as an office; she signed a cheque and he patted her on the shoulder, which he had never done before and he said she was always just the same. And Billy knew that he had patted her shoulder and said the words because it wasn't true and he could see that she was changed: older and run down. He didn't refer to David, or ask about any of her friends and she felt grateful and would have liked to have shown it, but became very practical instead. It flashed across her mind that the best relationship a woman could have with a man was when there was no thought of making love, or any amorous overtures, but with a man intent upon his skilled work: a carpenter for example.

'So why are we always itching for sex, when the best relations are not with each other's bodies but with things: ropes, stitching sails, planing wood, chipping stone?' But though she asked herself this question, she knew that it was not a fair one and that there was an answer in the shape of Madame Thomas and of Sam—only Sam. . . .

Monsieur Thomas helped carry her bags on board and shook hands. Then she started the auxiliary engine and he walked back and she watched him. Good man! He never turned his head, or waved, and she felt that was a proof of how well they knew each other.

Soon she had the *Connie* under sail and was out at sea.

The wind was bitingly cold. She put on a heavy duffle coat and an oilskin over that, and tied her sou'wester under her chin and then tied it down with a scarf which she wound round her neck. And then she sat motionless for an hour or two, only touching the tiller just occasionally. The sun had set. It grew cold, very cold. She put on the lights and went back to her place. And suddenly what had been hidden from her ever since Sam had suggested her holiday, what had made her voice tremble in Monsieur Thomas's little office, rose from her unconscious and became clear. She could never sail *Connie* again. It wasn't possible, it wasn't safe for her to be alone on her. David was there all the time.

His limp body lying there on the deck, the long fight to get him to breathe again, sleeping with her naked body trying to warm him and waking to find him looking at her body under the blanket in secret. Touching him, his young cock, the weeks of happiness. And all lost and over, as though it had never happened.

'I won't, I won't, I won't. . . .' she said aloud and clamped her jaws. 'It wouldn't be fair on Sam. I'd do it this minute otherwise.' She meant that she would jump overboard and let *Connie* go sailing on alone. Anyway she would wait and have some whisky and try and warm up. Going overboard and watching *Connie* sailing on, getting smaller and smaller, losing sight of her when she was in the trough of a wave and then catching a last glimpse of her lights before she went down into the dark sea. . . . It was a change to think about that, instead of David and his body all the time.

She went below, switched on the lights and looking for

whisky and water, found a pair of David's trousers stuffed in among the bottles. Monsieur Thomas must have picked them up and used them to prevent the bottles rattling. They had been white duck trousers but were very dirty with spots of tar, and stained with wine and there was a hole that she remembered on the right buttock, worn by the knife she had given David which he always carried in his hip pocket. If she cut the trousers up they would do for rag. She buried her face in them, felt something hard and, investigating, found the French knife with a horn handle, that she had given David. She remembered, then, that he had missed it after they had left the boat and that she had meant to buy another one, after she had given hers to him. What a beautiful object it was. Perfect with its one large blade, a spike lying beside the blade and a corkscrew on the back. Made at La Guiole in the Massif Central. She looked at it with loving eyes, opened the blade and shut it again, and slipped it into her pocket. Then she mixed herself a stiff whisky and water, took a gulp and set it down. Her thoughts went back. She had let herself in for something unbearable in coming back to sail the *Connie*. Why had not Sam, who knew everything, guessed what it would mean? But perhaps he had foreseen it and thought that she would go overboard and that that was the best way out. Perhaps he had meant her to: out of kindness because he had seen how unhappy she was. She realized, as she thought of this, that she was deceiving herself. She was trying to justify going overboard by putting the decision on Sam. It was a coward's thought. And why bring Sam in?

'Well I'm not going to. Not yet anyway.'

Connie gave a violent lurch and some water came aboard. If she didn't look out she would drown anyway. She rushed on deck, grabbed the tiller and got *Connie* on her course again. If there had been a storm and danger, she could have taken advantage of it. But it was a steady sea, boring, wave after wave, and cold as sin. She looked with disgust at the night and then put the helm up and headed back for Monaco. It was a head wind. She went below and brought the bottle of whisky up. Then, although she kept drinking, she began shivering with the cold and felt rather sick. Presently she began talking to herself.

'I know it's all my fault, David. I know that. I haven't any reproaches. I was damned lucky to get what I did. And what damned luck it was I got you breathing again. Suppose you had died on me then. I'm old and you're young and you'll live your life—I won't, I won't, I won't,' meaning this time that she would not give way to jealousy and self-pity. She drank more whisky.

'It's not your fault either,' she said addressing the boat. 'You're a beauty, a real beauty. I'm lucky to have had you and I love you, even though I can't sail you any more. You are sacred. I won't sell you ever.' A wave of maudlin self-pity came over her and she brushed away tears with the back of her hand, then drank more.

A little later she shook her head angrily and said aloud:

'Don't be so bloody silly. You're like Victoria after Albert's death.' She looked at the bottle. It was less than half full.

'I'm drunk. Well I may as well make a job of it,' and poured out more. The sea had got up and she had to steer all the time, even after she had rolled up a reef. It was dawn and she was like a figure of stone by the time she had made the harbour at Monaco. She made fast to a buoy, tumbled down into the cabin and fell asleep. It was past midday when she woke up. She washed, spent some time brushing her hair, changed her clothes, putting on a skirt as her trousers had got filthy, made coffee and ate a good breakfast, before she began packing her bags, cleaning up and making all shipshape, before going ashore. Then she left a note for Monsieur Thomas, who was away, fetched her car, collected her bags and drove off, heading for Nice, and then taking the road to Draguinon. It was lighting up time before she got on to it. She felt a bit scared and happy. Scared because she knew that she had been very near jumping overboard and happy because, since she had got into her car, she had stopped feeling like an automaton and was enjoying being alive. She felt rather like a naughty child that has escaped.

'I won't go and stay at Les Oursins. I won't see Moya or Felix or any of that crowd. And I won't ring up Sam.'

She drove slowly and stopped, when she felt hungry, to eat in a wayside restaurant. She was in two minds about asking for a room, but went back to her car instead. It would be more fun to be alone. She drove on, then found a little by-road that took her up a mountain and halfway down again, and finally she pulled off the road behind some bushes. Then she took her bags out of the back of the mini-traveller and made herself a bed with coats and climbed in. It was pretty hard, but she fell asleep almost at once and went on sleeping until she was woken by a peasant grumbling and calling out on the other side of some bushes. The sun was already up some way. She was stiff and cramped and stretched herself and went to look. The peasant was quite close to her in the next field, throwing dung out of a long narrow cart while his patient oxen stood waiting as though they would wait for ever. Then the man called, more gently to them this time, and laid his long wand of hazel over their backs and they moved on a few yards. Billy was delighted. She felt free. Everything was good.

'To think that I wanted to drown myself. I must have been mad. I am cured now.' The smell of the freshly turned over dung came in a breath of wind and she breathed it in, loving it because it was so strong and everything in life was good.

But not the coffee she was given in the next village. It was brewed of pure chicory and was vile, tasting at the same time stale and bitter. She added two more bricks of fly-blown sugar and gulped it down.

It was not until she was twenty miles along the road that Billy wondered where she was going. And it occurred to her that she might, in two days' time, call in at the Château de Berri and see Alamein. She scarcely knew her, but she had always been attracted by her and St. Clair de Beaumont was a nice man in his preposterous way. A change from Swiss bankers and British economists anyway. Then there was Dr. Matthieu Robert, who had been Sam's greatest friend during the war.

Next morning she stopped in Dijon to buy a picnic lunch and, at a greengrocer's, was seduced into buying herself a melon. It was the first one she had seen in France and must have been imported from Morocco, or perhaps Israel. She left the main road and drove on until about one o'clock when she came to a bridge over a stream with a cart track running beside it and, on the other side, a forest. She drove along enchanted by the place until she came to an old tumble-down water-mill with the mill-race rushing noisily in a miniature waterfall. The sun was quite hot; there was wind. It was enchanting and she settled down to eat her lunch on a sloping bank below the wall of the old mill. She had finished eating her salami and bread, and had stuck the point of David's knife into the melon, then, above the deafening roar of the water, she heard a sound and looked up. A man was standing just in front of her with a most unpleasant grin on his face. And, as she looked at him he opened his fly buttons and pulled out his cock and holding it in his hand he shook it at her and said something in a French she didn't understand, or perhaps it was Algerian, for he was dark.

Billy felt outraged and far more disgusted and insulted than she would have thought possible. It was not the sight of his cock. It was the horrible grin on his face.

'*Foutez le camp espèce de salaud obscène,*' she shouted at him and, at her words, he threw himself on top of her, holding her down by the neck with one hand and tearing at her tights with the other. She tried to throw him off, but he was surprisingly strong and they wrestled for a little, rolling sideways down the bank. He was strangling her and she knew she was near a black-out. And then suddenly she felt the round melon under her thigh and got hold of David's knife and pulled it out and jabbed the man with it. He recoiled, letting go of her neck and she jabbed the knife as hard as she could into his face. The point of the knife went into his mouth and the sharp blade sliced open the side of his lip and the corner of his moustache. He leapt back with mouth all blood and Billy jumped up and flew at him, with the knife in her hand. He turned and ran, but not before she had ripped the shoulder of his jacket. She stopped then, and he turned and began spitting blood and leaning against a tree.

Billy walked to her car and there, propped up against it, was a bicycle. The man was holding his jaw and watching her. It was not a new machine, but she hoped he valued it, so she wheeled it to the edge of the millrace and threw it down into the deepest part of the pool. He was still watching her as she gathered up her things, got into the car, turned it round and drove off. When she had got out into the road, she remembered that she had left her melon behind. She stopped the car and nearly went back for it, but wisdom prevailed. But when she started the car up again she was trembling so that she could scarcely hold the wheel and she found she was driving on the wrong side of the road. She pulled over to the right, drove on a few kilometres and stopped and rested and unexpectedly dropped off to sleep.

Afterwards she never told anyone about what had happened, but she saw the man's grin again in nightmares.

CHAPTER SEVEN

NEXT day Billy stopped her car in the drive in the wood that led to the Château de Berri. Inside the wood, among the brown oak leaves, were snowdrops, growing singly and in large patches, like snow drifted among the trees. Billy stopped the engine and got out and just because it was out of character for her to pick flowers, she picked one snowdrop and looked at it closely. She picked it because unconsciously she was trying to be someone else and not Lady Billy Tonson, *née* Lady Billy Flint, the tough sailor woman who had stabbed a man only the day before.

She examined the flower carefully, seeing for the first time its intense individuality and realizing that the flower in her hand was alive, a living creature entirely occupied in being a green-veined snowdrop, just as a little French boy is intent on growing up to be a Frenchman. She was still looking into the green-edged bell of the snowdrop and wondering about it, and at the back of her mind wondering why children always liked to pick flowers, even though they dropped them afterwards, when she heard a blackbird singing. She did not have to wonder why he sang. She knew and he brought back what she wanted to forget. Then there was the sound of a car coming down the drive behind her and stopping, because her car was blocking the way.

Alamein got out of the car and seeing Billy just inside the wood went up to her. She was gay, obviously delighted to see Billy and for some reason did not seem surprised. What green eyes she had got!

'You've been picking snowdrops—and I have just been thinking about you.'

'I've picked one. I have never really looked closely at one and felt that I understood it before,' said Billy.

'How marvellous of you to come. You'll stay of course. I'm all alone, Amadeo has gone to London but I'm expecting him back tomorrow.'

'And St. Clair?' asked Billy. She wanted to talk about the snowdrop, but it had been brushed aside.

'St. Clair is in Paris for the rest of the month.' And to Billy's surprise, Alamein put her arms on her shoulders and kissed her. They drove their cars to the Château and Alamein carried her shopping basket with a long loaf of bread in one hand and with the other tried to take possession of Billy's bag and in the polite struggle the long loaf of bread fell on to the floor, so Alamein had to allow Billy to carry her own bag.

She was given the room overlooking the garden and had a hot bath and changed her clothes and spent the rest of the morning talking to Alamein in the kitchen, peeling the skins off cold golden yellow boiled potatoes and slicing them up for a salad, while Alamein stirred up a mayonnaise and Billy asked questions about the family of the Beaumonts.

'Father is a rich man. He has just sold the film rights of his autobiography and it will be marvellous film—a story of adventures unlike any ever known in history. During the first world war he seduced Mata Hari when he was seventeen, discovered that she was a German spy who carried a secret code in an anklet she wore, fell desperately in love with her, but denounced her and sent her to her death. His first grey hairs appeared as she went to the firing squad. Later on he discovered that she was innocent and murdered the French Colonel who had framed her.'

Alamein went into fits of laughter.

'And how does Leela like it? Is she in Paris too?' Alamein stopped laughing and shrugged her shoulders.

'Father has behaved abominably to her. Luckily it's none of my business. But directly he became a rich man he threw her over. She has got a job as housekeeper to a retired Admiral in Brittany, a very pious man who makes her go to mass several times a week. St. Clair now has all sorts of fashionable women in smart society as his mistresses. I don't keep track. He brought an American Princess, married to an Italian Prince, down here once, but it rained all the time and she made a pass at Amadeo and left early. . . .'

After lunch Billy went to her room and fell asleep. She did not wake until it was dark. For dinner Alamein opened a bottle of St. Clair's best Corton and to her surprise Billy found herself telling Alamein all about David: how he had been sent to her uninvited, how she had taught him to dive with an aqualung; then how he had nearly been drowned and the agony and difficulty of dragging his unconscious body out of the water.

'I suppose it was after that that I made my mistake. I felt

that because I had saved his life he belonged to me. I ought to have learned from Sam that possessiveness is always destructive. And then I made an even more hideous mistake: I watched him.' And Billy described going to the National Gallery and how David and Gundred had come in and that David had detected her.

'It's because of that afternoon that he won't see me now.' There was a glow in Alamein's face. She filled Billy's glass again and said: 'You make it sound very horrible and it must have been for you. But you are quite likely making a mistake. Half the time one turns out to be wrong about what people are feeling. At least that has been my experience in life.' The two women went on sipping prune and talking late and when Billy went to bed she was rather tipsy and more comforted than she had been for many months. She thought that perhaps Alamein was right. She would see how things looked in the morning and perhaps not go back to London at all. She fell into a dreamless sleep.

Next morning she was still full of optimism, but determined to push on and explore France. So she packed her bag and put it in her car and, as it was a lovely spring morning, went out for a long walk—first along a path by the river and then, climbing up hill, to the site of an old castle where Alamein's mother's family had lived for centuries.

When she got back to the château there was a car unlike any she had seen before, standing in the yard. Amadeo Severin had returned.

She did not meet him until just before lunch, when she

was drinking a vermouth and gin with Alamein. He was tall and slim, fair and blue-eyed, quite unlike an Italian and said gaily:

'I spent last night at your house in Belgrave Square sitting up late with Sam. His new protégé was there: a boy called David Bruin. Sam thinks he's intelligent, but he has such odd opinions. Some people would call him a fascist. But he's not exactly that. Do tell me something about him?'

During this speech Billy had stood petrified with her glass in her hand.

What was she being told? That David had gone to see Sam? David must have come back looking for her, and they thought she was at sea and could not communicate with her. That must be it. She must dash back at once.

She realized that Amadeo was looking at her, expecting her to answer his question. 'I don't think I can really,' she said. Alamein came back into the room to say that lunch was ready.

'I'm terribly sorry. I must get back at once. I want to catch the first plane,' Billy hardly knew what she was saying.

Then she gazed rapturously at Amadeo and said:

'You don't understand. But it's too wonderful what you've told me.'

Then turning to Alamein she said: 'Forgive me bolting like this, but you understand,' and kissed her and ran down to her car and drove off.

Billy let herself into the house with her key: there was no one visible, but when she burst into the library, she

III

found Sam reading. He looked up from his book, not surprised to see her.

'Where's David?' she asked. Then as Sam looked at her in a curious way, she said: 'Amadeo Severin told me that he met David here. I suppose he had come to see me. And you thought that I was on the *Connie*.'

'I certainly thought that you were on the *Connie* until Alamein rang up to say that you were on your way here.'

Sam paused while Billy waited expectantly and, watching him, a sudden chill seized her even before he spoke and everything seemed unreal as she heard Sam say: 'I am sorry, my dear, but David didn't come to see you.'

'What did he come for then? What had he to tell you?' asked Billy.

'He hadn't anything to tell me, as you put it. I asked him here because I wanted him to meet Amadeo. I thought that they would interest each other. I believe they did. I thought you were miles away out at sea. It never occurred to me that you might visit the Château de Berri and hear of David's visit and put the wrong construction on it.'

'I still don't understand. What has been going on behind my back?'

Sam showed a faint sign of impatience.

'Nothing has been going on behind your back. David has not mentioned your name to me and I have not spoken of you to him.'

Billy glared at him. 'You are hiding something. You are trying to treat me as a child. You persuaded me to go away and, when you thought I was safely out at sea, you start seeing David. I'm not a complete fool. You must tell me the truth.'

Sam looked very tired. He paused and said:

'I have seen David quite a number of times because he has asked to see me. He has wanted to discuss various ideas he has and I think I am the only man he knows whose criticism he values. Except that I took care that you and he should not meet accidentally, which I thought would upset you, our meetings have had nothing to do with your being in love with him.'

'Do you really expect me to believe that?' asked Billy.

'Yes I do,' said Sam. 'David is violently against the student movement in the Universities. He thinks that the strikes and demonstrations and sit-ins should be put down by force and the students involved expelled. I take, as you know, a more liberal attitude.'

'Why did Alamein ring you up? So as to get David out of the house before I got back, I suppose.' She was suddenly beside herself with rage that Alamein, in whom she had confided, and whom she had trusted should have warned Sam that she was on her way home. She felt alone, surrounded by a conspiracy that she could not fathom.

'I don't believe a word that you've been saying. It's all blah, blah, blah,' she said with her voice breaking.

'That isn't like you, Billy,' said Sam. He got up slowly, out of his chair, tall, stooping, slightly pot-bellied, and went and took a tape out of a cabinet and put in on the record player in the corner of the room. 'David and I have had long discussions and I thought it would be interesting to record one of them.'

Billy stood biting her lips, bewildered and Sam bent down, put on the tape, switched on the instrument and at once David's voice, sounding rather conceited and amused and inappropriate to what Billy was feeling, filled the room:

'I would rather be a young communist, suckled in a creed outworn than any of my fellow students claiming what they call their rights before they have acquired a smattering of education: parasites on society, organizing violence before they have the knowledge to form rational opinions on any subject. Those who will not accept the discipline of work are useless drones and should be driven out of the hive and left to starve. Yes, starve, until they can feed themselves. . . .'

'Oh turn it off, turn it off,' cried Billy and, as Sam did so, she collapsed, throwing herself on the sofa.

Sam lowered himself on to the edge of the sofa beside her, put his arms round her and comforted her in murmurs.

'You must be patient, darling. I know that he is very fond of you.' After an interval he said, 'David is quite a remarkable boy. He has a remarkably clear head for his age. And what makes me believe in him is that he always goes against the popular trend of opinion. Even though I disagree with him on almost everything. He's a bit hard, but he will soften with time.'

Sam got up and fetched a decanter and two glasses.

'You had better have some whisky.' As she was drinking, he asked: What I don't understand is why you turned up at the Château de Berri when I thought you were sailing far out in the Mediterranean?'

' I shall never sail the *Connie* again. I can't bear it. She is full of David. She's haunted. His ghost is on board. If I hadn't thought it might upset you, I would have gone overboard. I nearly did and I wish I had now. I shall die of shame.'

Sam had gone back to his chair. He put his hands over his face as though to hide something too hideous.

'That had not occurred to me,' he said. 'Please forgive me, Billy, for making so many mistakes. You know that I did not intend to hurt you. But I have been unimaginative.'

'We all make mistakes all the time. It was what Alamein was saying to me last night. And my mistakes are a thousand times worse than yours and less forgivable, but I am the only one that suffers by them.'

Sam filled up both their glasses. Then he said:

'I used to think that having no active sexual life and no desire left, I should be less likely to make mistakes about personal feelings, because I am simply an observer. But it looks as though it wasn't true.'

It was the first time for many years that Sam had spoken about his impotence. It affected Billy strangely and out of cowardice she tried to keep the conversation abstract and intellectual.

'I suppose it flattens out the contours. Not experiencing passion minimizes your understanding of the strength of the obsession, yet at the same time it makes it possible for you to see the whole relationship far more clearly than the parties concerned.'

Sam looked at her and she saw that he knew that she had

115

spoken like that because she was dodging an issue that was too personal and too painful. She was not ready to help him, as he was helping her. Some time she must not dodge it, for, by dodging, she was betraying him.

'Are you going on seeing David without telling me?' she asked.

'As to my seeing him, it depends on him. As to my telling you, do you think you'll feel happier if I say: "I'm meeting David, so I shall be dining at the Club this evening?" Won't it make it more difficult for you waiting.'

'What do you mean by waiting?'

'Waiting until he wants to resume relations of some sort with you.'

'He never will.'

'Nonsense. People always do.'

After her return, Billy lived her ordinary life in London. Sam made fewer demands on her. He often dined out, but he never told her whether he would be seeing David or not. Once when he was out and she had drunk a good deal of whisky alone, she went to the library and found the record that Sam had made of the discussion with David. She played it over, but after the first sentences she could not have said what they were talking about. She sat staring at the machine, hating it, but when the record was finished she put it on again. Then, when she looked up, she saw that Sam had come into the room. He seemed rather fussy with his black bag locked full of papers and perhaps, she thought, rather put out by finding her there. He made her feel like a child doing something forbidden, though of course she had a right to play the record if she chose. The feeling of being caught was not helped by Sam asking: 'Do you agree with him or with me?'

'I don't know. I don't know. I didn't listen to what you were saying. I only wanted to hear his voice,' said Billy angrily. Sam stooped and stopped the record. He did not attempt to console her, but unlocked his bag and took out his papers. Billy got up and went out of the room in despair and then wished she had brought the whisky with her. She wanted some more badly, but did not like to go back, because she knew Sam was irritated. Finally she went down to the cellar and brought out another bottle of Grants. Irritation was so foreign to Sam, that she wondered if he were ill. But perhaps Sam was not ill, but was seeing her as she really was, she thought. In which case his love was over. 'Because nobody could love me if they really knew what I am like. . . .' She took a mouthful. How good it tasted. 'But Sam's love is such an extraordinary kind, if you can call it love,' she reflected. 'He used to be wildly adventurous as a young man. And then insanely courageous during the war. Getting in to a German concentration camp, in order to write a report on it and getting out again. And at last they caught him and broke him up. . . . I think he only loves me because he somehow enjoys the life of the body by proxy, through me. A *voyeur* and I'm the peephole through which he looks.'

And, for the first time since she had married Sam, she felt a touch of disgust at Sam's love, so gentle, wise and insistent. And their life together seemed *macabre*. The idea of going away—of leaving Sam—came to her and she was surprised to feel attracted by the idea of escaping from him, of living without his support, without a tie in the world.

'What depths of treachery am I capable of?' she asked herself and dismissed the idea. She must ring Harrods in the morning.

'And I'd be without Sam's money either,' she admitted to herself later, as she was undressing before going to bed.

'That wouldn't be so good. You wouldn't like that would you, you treacherous old whore?' she said looking at her naked body in the long glass.

'But honestly, I should be bored without Sam,' she said before she fell asleep. 'We've got so that we depend on each other.'

CHAPTER EIGHT

A FORTNIGHT later Sam handed Billy a letter he had written to David and the reply.

Dear David,

The doctors seem to think that a few weeks in a warm climate will restore me to vigorous health. I am therefore trying to persuade Billy to come with me to the South of France and, after that, perhaps to Italy. She doesn't want to come but I think that if you would join us, she would change her mind, because I know that she is longing to see you. So I hope you will agree to join us. There is no one, leaving Billy out of account, whom I would rather have as a companion and I am sure we could have lots of fun and see some lovely places. I shall be going by car and so you won't have any travel expenses. Also I want to discuss your ideas with you.

Yours,
Sam.

Dear Sir Samuel,

Thank you very much. I should love to come with you. Of course I should like to see Billy again, if she comes with us. I would rather pay for myself, but we can arrange that. Please give Billy my love and tell her

that I am also longing to see her. I did well in the exams
and I think that I shall get a grant to go either to Cambridge or to Sussex.

> Yours,
> David.

Billy read the letters carefully, made a sudden gesture and
then read them both again.

'Why did you ask David, Sam? Do you really want him?
Or is it for my sake?'

'Yes, Billy. It is all for your sake.' Then as she looked at
him with desperation, he said: 'What a goose you are. You
know that I am happiest when you are happy. And now
when I succeed in arranging something that will make you
happy, you can't take it simply and accept it.' She turned
her face away and he went on: 'You said that you hated
complications. So why make them? Remember that you
promised me to accept life.'

'I can't. I can't accept myself. Don't you see that I can't
believe that anyone could really love me? He ran away
from me because he saw that I was horrible, and if he
comes back he will only make me more unhappy because
I know that he'll run away again. And it's right that he
should. Besides, if he's there with us, I shall want to make
love to him.'

'Of course.'

'But it's not the right thing for him. His instinct is right.
But I can't help it and I shall easily seduce him. I'm not the
right person. And what sort of a holiday will it be for
you?'

'I expect I shall get along all right if you are there to take the young man off my hands occasionally' said Sam.

'Why do you do this? Do you really like him?'

'You can't expect me to feel the way you do about him. But he is intelligent. He has impressed me and I shall do what I can to help him along. And, as your lover, he's the best of the bunch so far.'

'You are a devil, Sam.'

'A devil? You sometimes call me a saint. But, anyway, you are coming.'

Billy nodded. Tears were in her eyes and she ran out of the room angrily. She could not have borne to impose the task of consoling her on Sam at that moment.

But, as soon as she was alone, she felt bursting with happiness. What did anything matter? Whether she was a monster, or not, when she would be driving through France with David beside her in a few days—and then tip-toeing off to his room when he had gone to bed.

But in these suppositions she was mistaken. When she came in from making her last purchases at Harrods the day before they were due to start, Sam told her that David had rung up to say that he would not be able to leave England with them. He had been summoned to an interview at Sussex University and it was an important one, as he thought he had failed at Cambridge. Sam had said that he could not postpone the trip and had booked David a ticket on Air France so that they could pick him up at Nice the morning after their arrival.

Sam had also fixed up that they should spend the first night at the Château de Berri.

Next morning Sam and Billy crossed by the Ferry and Billy drove Sam's big Bentley along the wet roads and reached the Château de Berri a little before sunset. It was the last day of April, nineteen sixty nine, and France was still stunned and drawing a breath of relief at the defeat of De Gaulle and his retirement to Colombey. The copse on each side of the private road that led to the château was full of wood anemones and the grass verge yellow with bands of cowslips.

The door of the château was thrown open as the Bentley drew up, and there was its master standing in the doorway—magnificently dressed in striped trousers, a braided black jacket, with a ribbon of the Legion of Honour in his buttonhole, a wing collar and the most remarkable patent leather button boots, with yellow suède insertions in their sides. It was clear that he must have been watching for them to arrive and had run down and flung open the door to greet them, as they drove up.

'There have been vast changes since you were here last, Sir Sam,' said St. Clair then taking Billy's hand and kissing it, before she was aware of what he was about.

'It all looks delightfully the same,' said Sam.

'The château remains in its pristine perfection,' drawled St. Clair. 'The transformation I refer to, is in the man you see before you. I, who was a neglected and impoverished exile, have become the leading figure in a renaissance of French literature. *Je suis Français*. And now that my old enemy the General has been beaten from the field, my position . . . But I will not expatiate. There are infinite possibilities.'

'I am glad that you think his defeat augers well,' said Sam.

'Sam is a bit worried, aren't you?—about the franc,' said Billy.

'I care nothing for the franc. I speak of the eternal values—the world of books and of the arts, of the creative imagination, of all that has made France truly great. But you must be tired. Let me take you to your room and tonight I will tell you of the part I have played in bringing about the defeat of the old tyrant.' He paused and added:

'There have been personal changes too . . . very sad ones. Leela, who was my support through the long years of adversity, has seized the opportunity to abandon me now that I am a wealthy man. The rats leave the luxury liners. . . . But you are too young to remember the *Titanic*.'

St. Clair shook his head mournfully: 'The poor dear woman is at Nantes, looking after the domestic problems of an Admiral—and from what I hear, his spiritual problems as well.'

He brushed up his moustaches and said gaily: 'Amadeo is at work in his laboratory and Alamein will soon be home. She is procuring a few delicacies for our fesat.'

'Tell me about the *Titanic*,' said Billy who was bristling with curiosity.

'During her trials the *Titanic* was full of rats. But none of them would sail on her maiden voyage. They were wiser than Sir Bruce Ismay.'

The taps of the bathroom ran cold and, when Billy went down to the kitchen to fetch a can of hot water, she found

St. Clair in his shirt sleeves and wearing an apron, busy in peeling the skins off boiled Jerusalem artichokes.

The feast, as St. Clair called it, had been cooked by him. It consisted of fillets of anchovy mashed up with Jerusalem artichokes with a sauce of mayonnaise and ground up tunny fish, liver and bacon with chip potatoes, and bread and cheese. There was no sign of Alamein's promised delicacies. But with two bottles of Côtes de Rhône it was quite a good meal.

The company of Doctor Robert and of Amadeo Severin whose research work greatly interested Sam, and of Alamein, to whom Billy had taken such a great liking, made it a happy party and St. Clair's fantasies were tolerated with good humour. Actually Billy thought Amadeo's account of his research, designed to prevent collisions between objects moving at very high speeds, was far more fantastic than any of St. Clair's intimations that it was his planning in political warfare that had led to the defeat of De Gaulle—and of the glorious future that awaited him in consequence, if he cared to embark on it. But he did not want to.

'I shall play no overt part in the future of my country. My work is literature. It is inevitable that I should be elected to the *Académie*. There is a movement to put me forward for the Nobel prize. But these are the mere trappings. I shall soon begin my work which is to be a counterblast to Jacques Elul's *La Technocratie*. But more of that anon.'

The wine was finished. The glasses of prune filled and refilled. Billy had not seen Sam in that happy mood for a long while. In London he was so busy that he was always on his own ground: she saw him during intervals in his work, knowing that he would be called back to it. He would switch off work and give all his attention and sympathy to her:—but the papers were accumulating which he would have to deal with before evening and, though he could appear to be unaware of them, she could not.

But here he was free and gave himself entirely to the young man, Amadeo, and to his old friend the boy's uncle. To St. Clair de Beaumont he had been deferential, with the result that after a few surprising statements, St. Clair had fallen silent. Dr. Robert was silent and observant: Sam and Amadeo talked.

Billy did not understand very much of what they said, but she was happy listening, for Sam was so intensely alive. In every sentence and question there was the gentleness, the absence of egoism, that was Sam, yet he was intent on nothing but the subject being discussed, with his mind cutting it like a razor.

The subject was—as far as Billy understood it—more fantastic than St. Clair's intimations of his own grandeur. It appeared that Amadeo was on the track of a discovery which would make collisions between rapidly moving objects impossible: from meteorites and spacecraft to jet liners and even bullets.

'I can already envisage a technique for objects moving with half the speed of light. It should be possible to apply some modification of it to supersonic speed. I doubt if it will ever be possible to cut down deaths on the roads.'

'What about collisions between stars and comets and so on?' asked Sam.

'I don't know whether they actually occur. There isn't much evidence. And, of course, the only ones we believe in happened a million years ago. I am only concerned with collisions much nearer home than the milky way.'

St. Clair rose and said: 'You must excuse me if I retire and say goodnight. Work of the utmost urgency has to be done before morning and like a rat without a tail "I'll do and I'll do and I'll do".'

He bowed to Billy, brushed up his moustaches, drew himself up to his full height and marched out of the room jauntily.

Dr. Robert went into fits of silent mirth; and said:

'*Le bonhomme se croit le Mirabeau de la nouvelle révolution française.*'

Billy was tired and knew that Sam ought to be in bed. He had had a long day and ought to take the greatest care not to exhaust himself. But when she said: 'It's time for us to go to bed too, Sam,' he shook his head and said: 'Run along Billy. There are a few more things I want to hear about from Amadeo. Matthieu can feel my pulse, if you insist.'

So Billy said goodnight and Alamein went with her.

Billy was asleep when Amadeo came into her room and said:

'Come quickly. Your husband has had a heart attack.'

Sam was lying on the sofa in the dining-room unconscious and Dr. Robert was bending over him. It was only a moment before Alamein came and then Amadeo drove

126

Matthieu to his surgery, to fetch whatever he thought necessary. It seemed an age to Billy before he returned, while she sat beside Sam just looking at him and unable to do anything. Matthieu had already loosened Sam's collar and he lay there just breathing, but making no movement.

After Dr. Robert had examined him he said that it was a stroke, a haemorrhage in the brain, and nothing to do with the heart. Alamein made up a bed in the drawing-room and Amadeo and the doctor shifted him to it, and Billy and Alamein undressed him. After that there was nothing to be done and Billy sat beside him holding his hand. It was limp and completely unresponsive. Alamein brought her a dressing-gown, as she was still in her pyjamas, and made her put it on. Later she lit a fire and brought her a cup of tea. Then she went away and Billy could hear her talking to St. Clair in the next room. After that she sat holding Sam's hand for a long time. She thought his breathing had stopped: the hand she was holding was cold and she was cold herself. Sam was dead and Matthieu came in, listened with a stethoscope and shook his head. He told her to go to bed herself, but she refused and stayed there until the dawn came. Then they had coffee in the next room and she went up to the bedroom and dressed and then she opened the front door and walked out. It was a marvellously beautiful morning, so Billy went for a walk through the wood, stopping to pick a bunch of cowslips and wood anemones and the first purple orchid that had thrust up through the dead leaves. During the day that followed, Billy could only completely realize that Sam was dead when she went into the drawing-room where he lay, and she saw that he was made of that sharp-featured, pallid grey material which takes the place of living human flesh. She felt very little and wondered why she did not feel more. She avoided them all, for she was afraid that if anyone spoke to her she would lose control of herself, though she knew that it didn't matter in the least whether she did or not. But when one of them came up and spoke she remained perfectly calm and answered their questions about what should be done.

Some time later St. Clair came to her and said that he would send for an undertaker and, unless she wanted to take the body back to England, he would like to offer a plot of ground for the grave at Bartas-les-pierres, beside the family vault in which his wife had been buried.

Sam always hated funerals and had arranged to have his body go to some hospital in England. 'But I suppose a French hospital would not want it,' said Billy.

'I'll see if Matthieu can arrange it,' replied St. Clair and went off to telephone to him.

When he came back, he said that a French medical school would be glad to accept the corpse, but that Billy and Matthieu would have to go and sign a paper in front of the mayor and have it witnessed by the *huissier*. Alamein drove Billy in to the little town, the paper was signed and witnessed and, late that evening, an ambulance drove up and Sam was put in it and driven away. Billy would have gone too, but Matthieu ordered her to bed and gave her an injection, in spite of her protests that she ought to go back to England and was quite well.

It was three o'clock in the afternoon next day when she woke up and had a bath—hot water had returned—dressed—and then with Alamein's help packed up her own and Sam's things.

She was saying good-bye and about to leave, when a taxi drove up and David Bruin got out. The first thing that she noticed was that he had grown his hair; it was parted in the middle and hung down on to his shoulders. Without waiting to greet his hosts, he went up and put his arms round Billy and kissed her.

'How did you get here?' she asked.

'I loved Sam. And I love you. I had to be with you.'

'I was just leaving,' said Billy.

But St. Clair had come up and taking David's hand said: 'You are the boy we call the screaming Adonis. I'm sure you don't mind our little joke,' for David was looking daggers at him.

'If only you had been here we could have had an Irish wake, with you keening in proper style for our dear friend.' Then by a happy association of ideas he added: 'It's not too late, I hope, to offer you a little whisky.'

'No thank you,' said David extremely stiffly and turned to greet Amadeo whom he knew.

An hour later they had said goodbye and driven off—together. 'Where are you going to?' asked David. Billy stopped the car. 'God knows. I suppose I'm going back to London. There'll be a fearful lot to decide and things to do.'

'Leave all that. Let's go off somewhere where we can be alone.'

'But you don't want to be alone with me really, do you, David? Isn't it just pity?'

'It's all I want—to be with you. As we were at first.'

'But you've got all sorts of things and people.'

'I'm quit of them all. I've wiped the slate clean.' There was a silence while Billy wondered if it were true and what the words meant.

'I suppose,' said David and hesitated.

'What were you going to say?'

'I suppose we couldn't go off together in the *Connie*?'

'But do you want to?'

'I think it's the best thing we could do. You can clean up in London at any time, later on.'

'The *Connie*'s had her refit. She's been laid up since I took her out, but we can put her in commission again without any trouble. It ought to be perfect down there at this time of year.'

'Let's go.'

'Won't it seem awfully cowardly—running away like this?' Billy asked.

'Who cares what it seems like—and to whom?' said David.

When Billy got out of the forest on to the main road, she stopped the car and hesitated. The road ran north and south.

'You know David. It's sweet of you and it's awfully tempting. But I ought to go back.'

'Do you think Sam would say you ought to go back— or that he would want you to go back? Can you imagine his asking you to, or expecting it of you?'

Billy did not answer, but a moment later she started up the Bentley and headed south.

They did not get far that night, but stopped at Prémery where the Bentley almost filled the little courtyard of the Hôtel de la Poste. Neither of them had eaten all day and the food that they were given seemed to them the most delicious they had ever been offered. After it they refused coffee and drank brandy and went to bed early. David held Billy close and his warm body consoled her and she wept and talked for a long time about Sam. Everything seemed to become clear in her mind as she talked. David did not interrupt her, but kept stroking her hair. She felt that for the moment at any rate he understood. And the gist of what she said to him was that she had been nothing but a wild animal, when she was a girl. Many men had loved her, but everything always went wrong in any personal relationship and it always left her believing that it was her fault and that she was unlovable. So she shot and swam and rode horses and got into fights with men. When she was twenty, after the war, she went to Brazil and lived with a mining engineer who beat her. And then he gave her the clap. She could not get it treated soon enough and had to have her ovaries out. Then she came back to England. As she spoke she felt David's muscles grow rigid and his nails dug into her shoulder. But she paid no attention and went on to tell him that she went on living the same racketty life, sailing boats in summer and riding in steeplechases in winter. Then, in nineteen fifty, she had met Sam and had fallen in love with him. He was the only man who had ever been good to her and she had repaid his goodness by constant infidelities and continual selfishness, but it made no difference; he always went on being good to her and loving her. And now it was too late for her to do anything about it.

After the storm of tears and hysteria that followed, David made her take two of the sleeping pills that Dr. Robert had given her and at last she fell asleep, with his arms holding her tight, feeling his young body close to hers.

CHAPTER NINE

NEXT morning Billy was half awakened by David pushing her body over, on to her side, away from him. She opened her eyes: it was dawn. David was sliding down into the bed, pushing her knees up and pushing his cock between her thighs until he had found the right opening. In her sleepy state, she felt him fumbling, and then woke up enough to help him a little and his cock slipped into her from the side and from below. He lay still, in her, for a long time and she almost fell asleep and then woke to a dream of pleasure.

He was making tiny movements, stiffening his cock and then letting it go slack and stiffening again and then he pressed it deeper, right in as far as it would go, and she felt herself open deep in to receive and grip the tip. She was content to let him explore her body. She was his, for him to do whatever he liked with. She was brimming over. He made more little movements and after a long time, while she slowly glowed with fire, she felt the spurt of his semen as he came. But he did not cry out. He said nothing, made no sound and she pretended still to be asleep. It had all passed in complete silence and there was something lovely and full of great sensuality in their not having spoken a word.

After a little while she knew from David's breathing that although his cock was still in erection and still deep in her, he was falling asleep.

She dozed off herself, thinking:

'I am his. For him to do whatever he wants with, whenever he pleases.'

They left Prémery late and stopped early to have a picnic in a wood, for the weather was fine and the sun warm.

Billy was astonished when David said to her: 'I would like to find that man and kill him.'

'What man?'

'That fellow whom you lived with in Brazil. Why didn't you kill him yourself?'

'Actually I might have done. But I was afraid to. And I am very glad I didn't. By the way I found your knife on board *Connie*. If you've still got mine, we had better exchange.'

They exchanged. 'Why do you want to change?' asked David as he pocketed his own knife. 'They are almost twins.'

'I don't know. I'm afraid of your knife. I might do someone an injury with it. I have never felt like that with mine.'

'Well, I would have killed that man if I could. And if he were here now, I would still kill him, though it was a long time ago.'

'You know, David, that Sam was tortured during the war. He was castrated. And afterwards, during the Nuremburg trials, he was called as a witness against the man who had done it. But he refused to testify, because after all the pain he had suffered, he didn't want to be responsible for more pain.'

'That was personal. He could forgive what had been done to himself. But I could not forgive what was done to you.'

They packed up their picnic things and went on.

That night they pulled off the Draguinon road, short of Grasse, and went up to a little hotel on the mountain side. They got a bad meal, as they were not expected, but they did not mind. After they had gone to bed, Billy said what she had felt it her duty to say, but had been putting off.

'You are being an angel to me and I know you love me and you know how much I love you. But there's no need for you to come on *Connie* with me. I shall go on a cruise anyway. But you have all your friends of your own age, and all your plans for the future. They can't be interrupted like this.'

She could not see David's face in the dark, but there was anger in his voice as he answered:

'How can you talk like that? I love you more than anyone. I feel you belong to me now. I ran away from you. And it is a good thing that I did. But now I have come back and I never want to see those friends as you call them—again. And they don't want to see me—I've broken with all of them entirely.'

'Not on my account, surely. That would be too absurd,' said Billy.

'No. Not on your account. Though Sam had something

to do with it, because he showed me an alternative to their way of life and how it was possible to live.'

'What made you prefer Sam's attitude to life?'

'Well he had an object in life, quite a lot of objects in life and he loved life and he spent most of his time working and doing things. Gundred and her friends sit up all night, smoke pot, or take l.s.d., live in chaos and never have regular work, or stick to regular plans. Of course I am a parasite on you at the moment, but that doesn't seem to matter because we are lovers. But it's not my plan of life. Their one idea is to get someone else to pay the bills, or else to leave them unpaid. To persuade some girl with a little money to pay until it is exhausted and then to find someone else. I would not mind their being dirty, idle and living in a state of frequent hallucination—but they have no intellectual criteria. They imagine they are superior to the rest of the working world. They never really learn anything thoroughly, never create anything, never really love anyone and never sacrifice the whim of the moment. They are the flower children without roots, flowers that fade soon and that the real world throws into the ashcan.'

David stopped talking. He was trembling with agitation.

Suddenly Billy realized that there was something else: that David was keeping something back.

'What is it?' she asked.

'Did Sam show you all my letters?' Billy shook her head. David looked surprised. Then he said: 'I'll explain it all later. I found out the reason and the cure. And I wrote to Sam and explained it all. And he said he thought I was right. You see I had found out all this and then Sam wrote to me, when I was longing to see you, but felt I had behaved too badly to do so.'

Billy kissed him and said: 'But they are awfully young. They'll grow out of it.'

'No. There are lots of them sponging along at thirty and forty who have never done a day's work in their lives. Some of them talk of making a revolution. Pah! If they can't empty their own garbage pails how can they clean up the slums of the world, or solve its problems? Sam really was altering the world, without most of its inhabitants realizing what was happening.'

David's contempt and fury with his own generation— or with the young people a few years older than himself— worried Billy. Obviously he had met the wrong sort of young people and he had met them in the first place through her. But where were the ones he should have met instead of them? And why, if he had broken with them, had he got long hair?

David interrupted her thoughts by continuing in much milder tones: 'Of course there are some of what you might call the Flower Children who have great charm of character and real virtues. They are kind people, they get immense enjoyment from nature. They live, some of them like gypsies, and are happy in a nomadic life. I spent a week-end with one lot who had horses. But they lack brains. Their minds are a hotch-potch of astrology, flying saucers, mysterious herbal medicines, having intercourse with "the little people"—that is with an older race who live underground in dolmens, buried under hollow green hills in Wales and Ireland, or they spend their time

dowsing with hazel twigs to find where the ancient Kings
buried their gold. One girl, I know, reads the future in the
clouds, I don't mean that it is going to rain tomorrow, but
what will happen next year.'

'It all sounds lovely to me, what would you prefer them
to be doing?' said Billy.

"Making real discoveries in the real world: trying to
find out why drones congregate in the same piece of sky
every year, as they are said to do. Find out why and how
young cuckoos migrate, why young English herons go for
a tour of Western Europe before they settle down in the
neighbourhood where they were hatched, why some
creatures can live on poison, or rapidly adapt themselves
to it. And all the mysteries about white ants waiting to be
solved.'

'You want them all to be naturalists?' asked Billy.

'Oh no. Those are just a few of the things we don't
know much about. There are thousands more, in physics
and chemistry.'

'I suppose we ought to know about everything,' said
Billy mournfully.

'Yes, we ought. In fact we must and we are going to,'
said David passionately.

'The world will be much duller when there are no
mysteries left,' said Billy.

'You wouldn't think that if you had cancer,' said David.

She could not think of an answer and the subject
dropped.

Billy waited for a day in the Monte Carlo hotel,
scarcely leaving it, telephoning to Sam's London office, to

his business associates and to her lawyers, and then waiting for long hours for them to call her—and then she had to wait another day, for documents to be flown out to her which required her signature and which had to be witnessed and legally attested.

'You might like to know about Sam's will, though a lawyer will read it to us tomorrow. He left me an income of five thousand a year tax free, which is a fearful lot. He left you a legacy of five thousand pounds and all the rest to Amadeo, for his experiments.'

In the intervals she made lists and sent David out to provision the *Connie* and get all ready for them to sail.

Meanwhile Sam's chauffeur flew out and took over the Bentley and drove it back to London. At last Billy was free, and she and David left the hotel and went on board in the dark. Suddenly she felt that she was alive and living. All the lawyers, managing directors, accountants, and bankers had been holding her in a net, so that she could not move. They wanted to drag her to London, to drape her in widow's weeds, to pin her down in her position. But now she had escaped. The tiny hull of the *Connie* was a world in itself, a world far larger than they would have allowed her. How good the touch of wood and the roughness of rope, after hotel carpets and cushions and lawyers papers.

They went below, had a drink—Billy a whisky—David a Chambéry Vermouth—and a piece of bread and cheese—and then went to bed lying squashed together in one bunk, silent and listening to the muted wash of a wavelet and feeling the *Connie* rocking ever so slightly.

David made love and Billy lay absolutely passive, letting the boy take his pleasure and herself at peace as she had not been for many months. After he had come with his cries and ecstasy and violent gasps for breath, she smiled in the darkness and stroked his neck and kissed him again and again. And after he had fallen asleep she went on smiling in the dark and sighed and fell asleep herself.

She got up, dressed and put to sea with the first light and the motor woke David, who came on deck. It was a dead calm and when they had hoisted the sails outside the harbour, they hung in folds.

At last the faintest breeze filled them and Billy stopped the motor and for hours they drifted, as much as sailed, leaving no wake behind.

By midday the breeze freshened a little and they put up a huge spinnaker and Billy set a course which would take them to the Balearic islands, for David had said: 'Why not go to Morocco?'

Billy planned therefore to put in at Alcudia for provisions and fresh water before going on to Tangier. After that—who could tell—they might go through the straits into the Atlantic.

The days passed idly, making slow progress, for there were a succession of flat calms unusual in that sea at that season. Late one afternoon they were lying side by side naked on the deck more than half asleep, when they were roused by the sound of something rushing through the sea. When they looked out, there was nothing to be seen but turbulent boiling in the water. Then, as they watched, they saw first one and then several dolphins playing about the ship, leaping one after another and disappearing. It was a game that they were playing: not a game with set rules, not hide and seek, or tag, but the joy of a game was there: the joy of showing off their strength, of sudden exertion and power, like horses chasing each other in a field and swerving suddenly away before they touched, or overtook each other.

Billy and David watched them with delight, but the rushing speed of the dolphins was so far beyond what they could possible achieve themselves, that they were not tempted to leap into the sea to join in: as well might a man on foot join in a horse race. Only after the party of dolphins had left them and finally disappeared, did David say: 'Oh to be one of them!' Billy said nothing and David said: 'You told me that night I got drunk, that I boasted that I was going to ride on a dolphin's back, like that boy in Pliny. I should need a firm seat to ride one of those.' After a pause David went on:

'Curiously enough, it was what I said when I was drunk that made Gundred interested in me. She even said she was going to do a painting of me riding a dolphin but of course she never got round to starting it. She drops everything because it's "an old story" before it's begun.'

Billy wondered if David had come back to her because he had been dropped as 'an old story'. It would be a mistake to ask him—but as the question stayed in her mind she suddenly blurted it out.

'You don't really think as badly as that of me, do you?' said David. 'You don't really think I'm washed about like a piece of floating seaweed? No. I came back to you because

I felt like one of those dolphins if it had been caught up in a sort of Sargasso Sea. And I shall stay just as long as I feel you are another dolphin.'

'Not simply from pity, for me?' asked Billy.

'I don't pity you particularly. I share your sorrow and Sam helped to bind us together, we love each other more because we loved him and, in different degrees, he loved us. Me as well as you.'

Billy was silent. Some things can never be said and she could never tell David that Sam was kind to him for her sake. And, as it was something that could not be spoken, she had already suppressed her own knowledge of it.

A week later Billy took up the subject of David's reference to Sam's way of life as a criterion by which to judge those of the young, whom he had so violently condemned.

'How do they fall short, more than everyone else, of what you feel you learned from Sam?'

'I can't compare the crowd I was talking about with Sam. There's no point of contact. But if I compare them with the masters at school, or with the butcher and the baker, they are inferior because they are rootless. They tell the same stories, drop the same names, live not for life itself, but just to get by.'

'You generalize a lot. Give an example,' said Billy.

'Take Deirdre, that lovely tall girl who is Gundred's great friend. She is intelligent, fascinating, she can be very funny. Her potentialities are much greater than yours, or mine. She could be an actress, a poet or a cook—each in the first rank. But she can't stick to one occupation, or to one man, for a month at a time. She isn't ever in love, but she has to have someone to tuck up with.'

'What's the explanation?' asked Billy.

'I think it's cowardice and a wrong set of values. She can't commit herself to an occupation, or to a man, because it would involve having to live according to certain standards.'

'As what?' asked Billy.

'Well—getting up in the morning—keeping her word, honesty, living not for the moment, but for the future.'

'I like living for the moment,' said Billy.

'No you don't. And Deirdre doesn't like it. She's bored and she's unhappy. To live for the day only is to condemn oneself to vacuity. It's only the certainty of what you are going to do tomorrow that makes today worth while. Life is a continuous experience, not a series if disconnected events, or perhaps I should say "happenings".'

After an interval Billy said: 'What you dislike in your generation is due to the atom bomb. You can't feel certain of what you are going to do tomorrow if there isn't going to be one. It is just that you are less imaginative than most of them.'

'Possibly. At any moment each of us may die. And in a hundred years, everyone now living on the earth will be dead. The atom bomb may mean that we all die at once, instead of one by one. On the other hand it may not turn out to be much worse than the black death, which wiped out three quarters of the population of England in the middle of the fourteenth century. But if it destroys life on the earth altogether, it is only doing what may happen at any time from an explosion in the sun, or a third ice age.'

'Isn't the horror, partly, that the future of mankind depends on the American President, or on some Russian or Chinaman about whom we know even less?' asked Billy.

'But the future of mankind has always depended on second-rate men—and criminals and crooks. And even if they do destroy us, I prefer to go on being myself till the last minute. So I think of the atom bomb as just another way of death. The fact that the *Connie* may sink tonight doesn't prevent us having this conversation. President Nixon doesn't stop me reading that book by Freddy Ayer.'

'I think you have missed out the most important thing about the atom bomb. However let's go back. Give me an example of what you object to in Gundred's friend.'

'No. I've said all that. But the reason for it is not that they are helpless in their environment. We all are. It's because the scale is wrong. And the men who can set the scale right are the architects and the civil engineers

'Look at the world today: giant roads like twisting ribbons thrown down on a child's toy country of fields and back yards. Vast cubes shooting into the sky: enormous aeroplanes, enormous plastic bags with enough oil in each to burn down a town, being towed through the sea, bursting and polluting it. Rockets landing on the moon. and the men who do these things live in tiny flats, termites in their galleries. The bigger their conquests over nature, the more restricted are their lives, and everything offered is sham: margarine instead of butter—tele instead of opera and theatre, powdered protein instead of rump steak. No wonder sensible people despair. I'm going to help to restore the balance; get the scale of human life right again. That's what I wrote to Sam.'

Their conversation was interrupted by a sudden change in the wind and with it a rapidly mounting sea.

'We must roll in a couple of reefs,' said Billy.

But the wind rose and it soon became necessary to get sail off *Connie*. By the time the mainsail was stowed away and the *Connie* left with nothing but the reefed staysail the sea had become mountainous. Soon it was dark. They ate a quick meal of biscuits and cheese and each drank a tumbler of whisky and water. Then David went to the tiller and Billy stretched out below. She had torn a fingernail in getting the mainsail down, but the annoyance of having done so, and the pain, did not prevent her rejoicing in what David had said. However their personal relationship might develop, David would come to no harm. He was safe from the malaise of his generation. And he was trustworthy. With David one would be safe. And she loved him: she adored him.

'Square or round or tetrahedral—he is the most wonderful creature in the world—and I am the luckiest woman alive.'

She fell asleep.

Billy was stretched out in her bunk and had wedged herself so she could not be thrown out. She was fully dressed, but barefoot, and had got deep into her sleeping bag, as it had turned very cold ever since the storm began.

She slept fitfully and was actually asleep when the *Connie* rolled right over on her side and the sea came in. It was pitch dark, for the electric light went, and by the time she had struggled out of the sleeping bag, she was waist deep in water. Then she was thrown head first on to the galley. She put out her arm to save herself, but the force with which she was thrown, broke her collar bone, broke her left thumb and dislocated her shoulder joint.

She scarcely noticed the pain, but became very angry when she found that her left arm was useless. Then she thought for a moment that she was fainting, but her rage saved her and taking advantage of another roll, she made the deck. It was much lighter: she could see David lashed in the cockpit, waist deep. The *Connie*, half full of water, wallowed between the seas that broke over her. Billy expected her to founder at any moment, but after each sea, she slowly rose again. Twice Billy was almost swept overboard, for she could only cling with one hand. The second time she only saved herself by gripping the standing rigging between her thighs. She reached David and she might have been carried away then, if he had not lashed her to himself. All her strength was gone. The noise of the storm was so great that though their heads were touching they could only make each other hear by shouts.

'Hit us suddenly, Didn't see it coming,' shouted David.

'Can't last much longer,' yelled Billy. She did not tell him that her left arm was useless and he was too much

146

occupied watching the seas and trying to hold the *Connie* head to wind, to notice her crippled way of clinging to him, with only her right arm. They stayed like that for a long time. It was bitterly cold. The dawn came swiftly and looking back over the stern, Billy saw the coast—a black line—less than a mile away. They were being driven on to a lee shore. It was Africa—probably Morocco. She noticed for the first time that the staysail had gone and that the dinghy had been carried away.

'We shall have to swim for it,' she shouted into David's ear. He looked round quickly at the coast line.

'We may make it before she goes,' he yelled.

'Each for himself, remember. We can't do anything to help each other in a sea like this,' shouted Billy. Then, as David didn't reply, she shouted again: 'Each for himself. You understand?' and he nodded.

The *Connie* was drifting fast and she would perhaps have reached the shore, but for a rock. Suddenly she hit, broached to and went down in a smother of foaming sea and if David had not pulled out his knife and cut the line, both he and she would have gone down with her when she rolled right over. As it was they were almost suffocating when they surfaced and were able to snatch a breath of air. Billy saw David get rid of his coat. But, with only one arm, there was no way for her to get her anorak over her head. Already David was swimming strongly, but Billy, forced to adopt a side stroke, could make little progress with her one arm. A roller lifted her high and she could see David, in a gap between the rocks, already close to the shore. A wave broke over him but in the distance she saw his black head come out, a pinpoint in a smother of foam. Then the great roller caught her, the undertow took hold of her, and the next wave smashed her with terrific violence on a rock.

THE END